~~Ollie's Collection of Cool St~~

STUF

~~Ollie's Kritter Squiddles: A Tentacular and~~
~~Authenticle Guide to the Universe~~

no too long

~~Ollie's Octrageously Ofahfah—~~

no

~~Ollie's Octrageously Official Omnicar~~

BUS! OMNIBUS!

OLLIE'S OCTRAGEOUSLY OFFICIAL OMNIBUS

Members of the Super
Secret Sages' Club

Name: Sloane Daniel Beaumont

Star Sign: Brael

Registered: Divine

Sagittarian: Touched by Starlight

Eye Color: brown

Hair Color: black

Features: big magical eyebrows

Starkiller, killed ~~a god~~ ~~two gods~~ idk man he's killed a whole bunch of gods okay? He's super badass :D

Parents, Daniel and Pandora, murdered in a bad ritual (and it was like right after Dhankes. Big bummer) :(

Former detective at the AVPD, worked with Milo & Uncle Chase doing magical enforcement stuff

Private Investigator – Beaumont Investigations. Very fancy card, has the Sage's Cross on it! :D

Married to Azaethoth the Lesser, one daughter named Pandora (AKA Panda Bear, Her Majesty Panda, The Pandariffic Princess, Pandora the Non-Flammable)

Name: Azaethoth the Lesser AKA Loch

Star Sign: Mondelo

Registered: N/A (uh, he's a god, so no)

Sagittarian: God of Tricksters, Thieves, and Divine Retribution

Eye Color: green

Hair Color: red

Features: tentacles of the bluish-gray variety

Brother of Tollmathan, Gronoch, Xhorlas, and Galgareth. Son of Salgumel, he who was spawned by Baub, the child of Zunnerath and Halandrach, they who were born of Etheril and Xarapharos, descended directly from Great Azaethoth himself

Named for his great-great-great-grandfather, Great Azaethoth

Really loves Gordon Ramsey and cooking

56 siblings (WHOA)

Is really a big giant dragon with cool shiny wings and loves taking things that don't belong to him

Name: Pandora Azaethoth the Lesser Junior Beaumont :D :D :D (so cute!!!)

Star Sign: Yerone

Registered: N/A

Sagittarian: Demi-goddess :D

Eye Color: brown

Hair Color: red

Features: Really reallyyyyyy likes fire

The adorable and super spunky daughter of Sloane and Azaethoth the Lesser <3<3<3

Was the result of Loch being a very "irresponsible god"

Likes applesauce

Hates green beans

Favorite words are "mass panic" and all the very bad ones she's totally not supposed to say

Born on the summer solstice from an egg that Sloane carried (godly pregnancies are crazy), she's growing super duper fast. Already walking and talking and ready to learn how to pick locks with daddy Loch! XD

Name: Tedward Beauseph Sturm

Star Sign: Molbrot

Registered: Air

Sagittarian: Babbeth's Tongue

Eye Color: green

Hair Color: brown

Features: Big AF

Worked at Crosby-Ayers Funeral Home as removal tech

Can totally see and speak to the dead (WTF YO)

He's your ex-boyfriend and you didn't know he saw dead people?
NO :(:(:(

Engaged to King Grell, so he's gonna be Asta's step-daddy, and oh yeah his little brother is Ell

Soul is bound to Graham, a little boy who drowned with Ted when he tried to save him at the beach. I was able to bring Ted back with my starsight and resurrect him, but I couldn't save Graham. :(:(:(

People used to call him Teddy or Teddy Bear because of his size (pretty sure he hated it)

Parents were both Lucian, but he learned a little bit about Sages from the funeral home

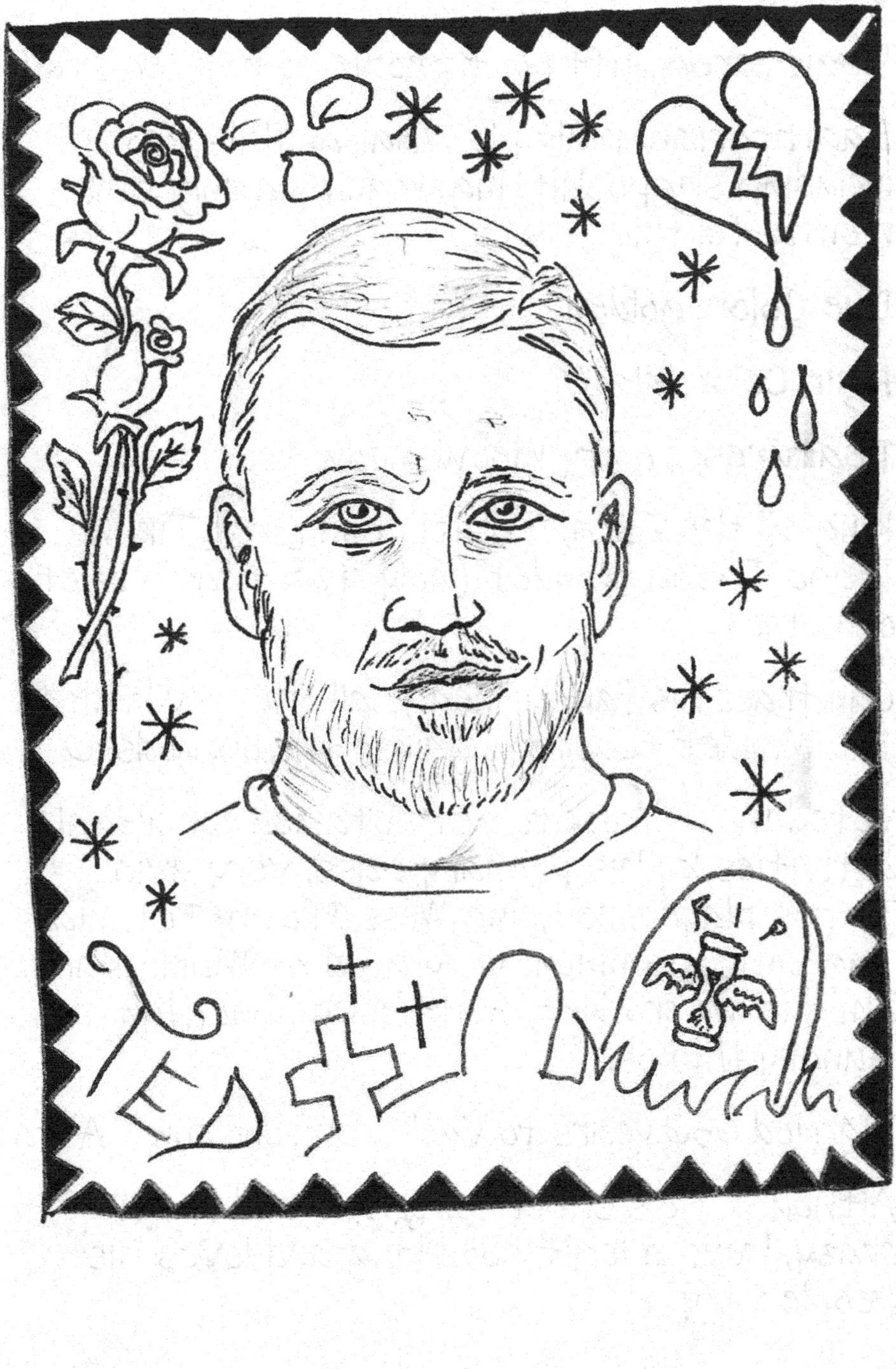
RIP

Name: King Grell

Star Sign: Atherael

Registered: kitty cat people do not register

Sagittarian: multiple magical abilities including shapeshifting, manipulating time, mental texting

Eye Color: golden

Hair Color: black

Features: pointy meow meow teeth

King of the Asra, Thiazi desu Grell Tirana Diago Tasha Mondet (holy crap that's a lot of name)

Can trace his family lineage all the way back to the Mondet Rebellion against the old gods :O

Voted most likely to get detained for illegal activities by his primary class, very avid Tetris player, reigning Miss Pretty Petunia Pageant Champion, very good at Mario Kart, amigurumi crochet, Battleship, and Hungry Hungry Hippos.

Married 656 years to Vael Crem, one son – Asta

Although he's super sarcastic and kinda crazy, he is a legit good king and loves his people very much

Name: Elwood Q. Chase

Star Sign: Baubel

Registered: Fire

Sagittarian: Shartorath's Hearth

Eye Color: blue

Hair Color: red

Features: his awesome long hair and brown fedora

Totally dating Gordoth (aka Gordoth the Slut) and he's super ridiculously happy and adorable <3

My uncle! :D :D :D (My father's older brother)

AVPD Detective, super awesome cook, might be the most messy person in the entire universe XD

Parents were kinda ~~agonal~~ agnostic but they did the conversion thing to be Sages before they died.

Always skips the second *Die Hard* movie

Bought his trusty fedora a few years ago right around the same time he met Merrick

Been a cop for like a million yearsssss
(idk he's old)

Name: Gordoth the Untouched AKA Merrick

Star Sign: Ernkael

Registered: Divine (well, his vessel was)

Sagittarian: God of Justice and Righteous Wrath

Eye Color: blue

Hair Color: black

Features: might have a stick up his butt idk Loch said something one time but yeah green tentacles

Super corny sense of humor, loves dopey puns

AVPD Detective, partners with Uncle Elwood and ahem romantic partners toooo <3<3<3

Benjamin Merrick was a detective that Gordoth admired and maybe he oops got him killed so took over his body to keep Merrick's legacy going!

Gordoth is Loch's uncle, one of Salgumel's brothers

Brother of Salgumel, Shartorath, Yeris, Ulgon, Elgrirath, Zarnorach, Xarbon, Solmach, Eb, Ebb. Ebbeth, and Lozathin, spawned by Baub, the child of Zunnerath and Halandrach, they who were born of Etheril and Xarapharos, descended directly from Great Azaethoth (these are always so long!)

Name: Milo Evans

Star Sign: Zitrone

Registered: Earth

Sagittarian: Ulgon's Roar

Eye Color: brown

Hair Color: black

Features: big fuzzy beard

Sloane's college bestie, met when he accidentally punched Sloane in the nose at a concert D:

Forensic Technician at AVPD

Dating Lynnette, expecting their first kiddo soon

(Very intense debate over the kiddo's name, but it's like something spacey and I don't remember what)

A recent convert to the Sagittarian faith thanks to Loch bopping him in the head with a tentacle, but he is dedicated and eager to learn everything he can to be a good Sage!

Mega-nerd who loves sci-fi and fantasy, totally loves to cosplay as his favorite characters :D

Name: Lochlain Fields

Star Sign: Atherael

Registered: N/A

Sagittarian: Yeris's Tears

Eye Color: green

Hair Color: red

Features: Super awesome thief, favorite devotee of Azaethoth the Lesser for stealing cool stuff

Looks just like Loch. Or Loch looks just like him. (But Lochlain is the fluffy sweet puppy version)

Sage's Cross tattooed on his chest

Married to Robert Edwards who is the Good Robert because Bad Robert Dorsey was actually possessed by Tollmathan and then got exploded.

Pretty well adjusted for someone who's died (hey like me! Although I guess I only died a little, He died, like, all the way off unplugged died :D)

Fields family has been Sagittarian for countless generations and they all live as rogue witches

Name: Lynnette Fields

Star Sign: Lithone

Registered: N/A

Sagittarian: Yeris's Tears

Eye Color: green

Hair Color: red

Features: Kickass necromancer

Dating Milo and expecting first crib critter soon :D

Lochlain's younger sister, used to be a waitress

Keeper of the Fields Family grimoire, a powerful collection of spells and rituals passed on through countless generations of Sages <3<3<3 (so cool!)

Bound Fred's soul to a wooden spoon to make him into a ghoul

AKA Snowflake :O (I think that's like a secret code name)

Big super nerd like Milo and also loves to dress up as her favorite characters. They met at a sci-fi con standing in line to meet the same actor from their favorite space action movie! :D :D :D

Name: Robert Edwards

Star Sign: Hurnkrone

Registered: Air

Sagittarian: Meuvothin's Touch

Eye Color: blue

Hair Color: blond

Features: left-handed :D

Married to Lochlain Fields! <3<3<3

Met when Lochlain needed to sell something that he stole and says it was love at first sight (aww that's so sweet!) <3<3<3

Runs a jewelry store that's a front for fencing illegal goodies. Got involved with black-market dealings because his grandpa was part of an underground group that helps ghouls. Ghouls need a lot of special and usually not legal magic to heal them, and Robert inherited the trade and sneaky contacts after he died.

Lived in the "broom closet" as many Sages do, i.e. hiding their true faith from people to avoid being ~~percussioned percussed persnickety~~ persecuted.

Name: Professor Emil Kunst

Star Sign: Hurnkrone

Registered: Divine

Sagittarian: Touched by Starlight

Eye Color: blue?

Hair Color: uh, round??

Features: Dead

Used to be a short frail old guy, but now he's a blue and round orb thing since Sloane killed him :D

Dated Sloane's mom in college, converted for her and became super obsessed with Sage history and started studying it

Royal Occult Advisor to His Majesty, King Grell of the Asra, Royal Historian, Official Record Keeper, ~~cheap plastic prognosticator~~

Tried to destroy an evil Salgumel totem like 20ish years ago with Sloane's mom and dad, but it went all kinds of wrong and they died. Kunst spent the rest of his life trying to destroy the totem for realsies, and offered his own life for Sloane to take as the fuel for the ritual. :D

Name: Fred Wilder

Star Sign: Baubel

Registered: N/A

Sagittarian: Baub's Rage

Eye Color: brown

Hair Color: black

Features: GHOUL AKA Hot Stuff :D :D :D

Real name is Farrokh (named after his maternal grandpa)

His mother was Tauri, a follower of an eastern religion that reveres the Sagittarian gods by different names and believes in a cycle of multiple lives via reincarnation

Parents died when he was super young and was unofficially adopted by the Fields family <3<3<3

Almost died in a fire when a heist went wrong, and Lynnette was able to bind his soul with a wooden spoon to a ghoul body to save his life :D

Dating Ell who is also his ghoul doc, and they are both super obsessed with this old epic fantasy TV show called *Legends of Darkness.*

Name: Elliam Jimantha Sturm

Star Sign: Molbrot

Registered: Void

Sagittarian: Silenced

Eye Color: blue

Hair Color: blond

Features: ghoul doctor, wears a scarf and gloves

Maybe he doesn't like germs? IDK he's like the one member of our club that I haven't met yet! (Drew him from a photo on Fred's phone because I'm sneaky) >:D

No, you're not. Fred absolutely saw you.

No he didn't. I'm a ninja.

You're as subtle as a sledgehammer.

NINJA! >:D Oh! And he's Ted's little adopted brother. Never met him when me and Ted were dating because they're all estrangled or something

Estranged.

He doesn't seem that strange. I hear he's real nice. :D Him and Fred having been dating for like everrrrrrr!

Name: Prince Asta

Star Sign: Lithone

Registered: kitty people are not registered

Sagittarian: Asra kitty cat person

Eye Color: golden

Hair Color: black

Features: also has pointy meow meow teeth

Son of King Grell and Queen Vael Crem, full name is Asta desu Crem Dianah Kane Bavar Nico Lucet

Is a "desu" like his father because they're both only children, and Asran names indicate birth order and family lines for all previous generations back to the beginning of their people

Has a form of starsight that allows him to see the future, called Great Azaethoth's Glimmer

Really loves the Backstreet Boys and Italian food

Is usually naked because of his frequent portaling and says the whoosh feels good on uh certain bits but still rocks sunglasses if he's hanging around on Aeon 'cause it's all bright and stuff --O_O--

Name: Urilith

Star Sign: Zitrone

Registered: N/A

Sagittarian: Goddess of Fertility and Children

Eye Color: varies depending on her vessel

Hair Color: idk she's hard to keep up with!

Features: bright yellow tentacle bits

Mother to Azaethoth and Galgareth and a whole bunch more, formerly the Goddess of Love

Has 102 children, 5 of them with Salgumel and the rest with other gods. Although she can totes spawn her own kids like any god, she chooses not to because "making them is half the fun"! XD XD

Was married to Galmelthar before Salgumel, and their union was traditionally the first of all the sexy times to start off the spring equinox party

They divorced because Galmelthar was unfaithful and some say the stars of Lithone are actually her tentacle rising up to punch him in the nads! XD

Name: Galgareth

Star Sign: Baubel

Registered: N/A

Sagittarian: Goddess of Night, Serendipity, and Love

Eye Color: blue

Hair Color: black and purple and blue ?? (varies because Toby, her chosen vessel, keeps changing it)

Features: lip, eyebrow, and nose piercings

Azaethoth's younger sister, daughter of Urilith and Salgumel, has big lavender tentacles

Even in the dreaming, Galgareth woke up every Winter Solstice to bless solstice flames and light one for Beltara, the first flame Beltara visits to light the stars of Great Azaethoth's crown

Chosen vessel is Toby, a young teenager who got into Sage stuff to piss off his neglectful parents and ended up being a Galgareth stan :D :D :D

Used to steal sacrifices and offerings from other gods' altars when her and Loch were young XD

Name: Jay Tintenfisch

Star Sign: Hurnkrone

Registered: Void

Sagittarian: Silenced

Eye Color: hazel

Hair Color: brown

Features: big glasses

IT tech at the AVPD (does everybody ever work there or is it just me!?)

Adopted Mr. Twigs who was really Asta in-kitty-nito

Former roomies with Ted, met at a funeral :D

Got into computers when he was a kid

Since he's Silenced, he always liked computers and learning programming 'cause it was like a kind of techno-magic he could actually do

Has a very complicated relationship with the Asran Prince, Asta (Like ooooo I think they were a thing but then they broke up oooooo!!!)

Name: Oleander Logue (that's me!)

Star Sign: Yerone

Registered: water

Sagittarian: I got starsight! :D

Eye Color: green

Hair Color: red

Features: Scar on chest from that one time I kinda died but then Uncle Chase saved me!

Starsight thingie lets me see all that is hidden and there is stuff that just should be hidden because omg nightmare fuel

I like art and painting and drawing stuff :D :D :D

My uncle is Elwood Q. Chase who is super awesome anddd my boyfriends are Alexander and Rota <3

Mom and Dad are Holly and James, I got two older sisters (fraternal twins!) named Amaranth and Juniper, but they moved for college forever ago

(okay plus we don't talk much cause uh all the drugs and stuff)

Was in art school for art but I dropped out >_> now I translate stuff using my cool nifty starsight powers!

Name: Alexander

Star Sign: Beltarael

Registered: Void

Sagittarian: Silenced

Eye Color: red

Hair Color: white

Features: ~~super hot and adorable, cute butt~~

STOP

~~Hundreds of binding symbols all over his body — and I do mean like all over him~~

STOP IT

Kidnapped after his parents were killed by the god Gronoch and subjected to years of super yucky experiments to bind his body with Rota's soul

~~Made out with Sloane one time~~

KEEP ME OUT OF YOUR BOOK

Parents were Milton and Dianne Ward, real name is Landon. Alexander is from LXIX, ID # assigned by Gronoch (which is all super sad and stuff, but the number is totally 69) XD

Loves pina coladas. Not so much getting caught in the rain :D

Name: Rota

Star Sign: Halrael

Registered: Not ~~appliqué~~ applicable

Sagittarian: God

Eye Color: Clear

Hair Color: Translucent

Features: See-Through (you get the idea)

Rota is the old god whose soul was bound to Alexander as a result of Gronoch's experiments

He does not know what god he is, and no one else seems to know either – not even other old gods (very suspish!!!)

Named himself from a big control dial he saw at Hazel Medical (think it said "rotate to open", but he couldn't actually read the whole thing)

Boyfriend to Alexander and meeeee <3 <3 <3

Absolutely loves horror movies, and he tries to figure out the ending (pssssst he's usually right because he's seen like every freakin' movie ever)

Name: Sullivan Jacob Stoker

Star Sign: Mondelo

Registered: Fire

Sagittarian: Jake the Gladsome

Eye Color: blue

Hair Color: dark, salt and peppery

Features: Cool widow's peak, black shiny tentacles

Son of Abigail the Starkiller and Zunnerath :D Has been hiding that he's totes a freakin' half-god hiding out in plain sight dun dun DUNNNN!!!

Super sneaky gangster who runs drugs and other bad things, but also has several legit businesses like Dead to Rites (a bar run by Sages), The Velvet Plank (an exotic dancy club), and Drusilla's (a sexy adult store)

Rules over the Hidden World, a secret place where descendants of the everlasting peeps can hide out

Has a kitty named Madame Sprinkles who is a very pretty shade of lime green (thanks to Loch)

Although he cannot summon a sword of starlight like Sloane, he can totally wield one 'cause Abigail is his mama and he has Starkiller juju

Star Signs

BAUBEL

(JANUARY 20 – FEBRUARY 18)

This constellation honors Baub's legendary Sweep of Zebulon, a time when he became so enraged by his godly family's mess that he made a broom out of a meteor shower and nearly tore apart their divine home. To appease him, Galmelthar made lemon beer to drink for a spiritual cleanse and got him too drunk to clean anymore.

Baubels are thoughtful and intellectual, and they can also be extremely stubborn. They pride themselves on being independent, but they do love excitement and meeting new people. They are known for being quite unpredictable, inventive, and may have an affinity for brooms. After all, a broom may be used to sweep or could be a makeshift weapon. Baubels like to be prepared for anything.

TODAY'S HOROSCOPE:

Today is the day that you clean your kitchen. Okay, maybe it's not your kitchen. Maybe it's your bathroom? I dunno, it's not that clear. I just know you really need to clean something, and it's, like, super gross. Fix that stuff. Now. It will make you feel better, I promise, and then you can do something really cool. Go read a book. Take a bath. Eat a big yummy meal. You deserve it. You sparkle.

Watch out for cats.

Not because anything bad is gonna happen, but just because cats are really cool and some of them are, like, super fluffy and cute. You might even be able to pet it.

Ask permission first. Just in case.

If you get scratched or bitten, that's totally not my fault.

ZITRONE

(FEBRUARY 19 – MARCH 20)

These stars are so named because the Sages believe them to be Galmelthar's mighty tentacle holding a lemon. Great Azaethoth presented the fruit to Galmelthar to commemorate the end of the very first spiritual cleansing, where it was said that all the gods got drunk off his lemon beer for a month and vomited profusely, thus beginning a long and sacred tradition.

Zitrones are emotional, sensitive, and intuitive. They're quite empathetic, often to a point of self-destruction, which leads some to avoid other people altogether and isolate themselves. Zitrones are known for being very romantic and expressive, though they can easily be just as selfish as they can be selfless. Like with lemons, how much sugar you add will determine the flavor of Zitrone you get.

TODAY'S HOROSCOPE:

Someone is going to upset you today. I'm super sorry about it, but it's just ~~enviable environmental~~ inevitable. Someone is gonna say or do something, and it's gonna suck in a not fun way. Take lots of deep breaths, run a hot bubble bath, and ignore them whenever it happens.

Your honey nut feelios are totally valid no matter what and know that you are really awesome, okay?

Words can be hard. Like, they can be pointy, and I know they can hurt, but do your super best to remember they're just words. You can write them all down and then erase them! If it makes you feel better, you could totally set them on fire too.

T~~HE~~ WORDS. The WORDS. Not the person. Don't set the person on fire. That's illegal.

LITHONE
(MARCH 21 – APRIL 19)

The constellation Lithone shows Urilith's tentacles rising out of the sky to greet Galmelthar's as they come together in the sky for the spring equinox. Their union was traditionally the first joining to start the fertility celebrations of Urilitha and would signal that spring had truly begun.

Lithones are daring, confident, and spirited. They're spontaneous and love adventures, but their passions can also manifest as rage. They are known for short tempers and sharper tongues, though they do not hold grudges for long. Be careful if you ever challenge a Lithone to a dare. Their fierce temperament will not let them back down, whether it's trying a new spicy food or being the first one to get naked for an orgy.

TODAY'S HOROSCOPE:

You are going to have a super amazing day because you're gonna make it amazing. No matter what happens or what life throws at you, you are gonna rock the crap out of it! And I know that you're up for anything, but maybe don't try any new sports or physical activities today.

I can see clumsy little gremlins, like, totally headed your way, so avoid that new aerobic pole dancing class or that hang-gliding adventure. Just for today at least. You can dance and glide around tomorrow, I promise. Use today to relax and be lazy or maybe try a new video game or something. That'll be safer.

Your lucky number is ten. I picked ten because that's how many fingers I have, and it seemed like a good number to pick for you.

Don't eat glue.

HALRAEL

(APRIL 20 – MAY 20)

Zunnerath and Halandrach's twisting tentacles are represented by this bright constellation. They controlled the weather of the world together, and Sages say these stars were once a single strand until Abigail the Starkiller killed Halandrach, causing the stars to split apart, never to be joined again.

Halrachs can be either a gentle spring or a wild hurricane. They make loyal friends, nasty enemies, and rarely anything in between. While loving and sensual, they can also be jealous and resentful. They value stability, loathe change, and this makes them both stubborn and reliable. Halrachs have a high appreciation for beauty and can be quite greedy though, so don't be surprised if one summons a sword of starlight and comes for your mate.

TODAY'S HOROSCOPE:

You're gonna enjoy something with sprinkles today! Yay! Wait, maybe you don't like sprinkles. Then you're not gonna enjoy it. I can definitely see sprinkles in your future though, uh, so, I hope you like them. It could be these are magical sprinkles, and they represent something colorful and sweet is gonna happen! That would be super cool.

Also, instead being super jelly over that cool thing you're being super jelly about, you should try getting one of your own. You're a super awesome person, and you deserve the cool thing too! Treat yourself. Treat, heh, like a treat with sprinkles!

Okay, but wait, only if the cool thing is not a person. You don't just get people. That's weird. And people are not treats. Technically.

ATHERAEL

(MAY 21 – JUNE 20)

Etheril and Xarapharos were the first of Great Azaethoth's godly children, and he put them in the stars to thank them for building the fire for the gods' summer solstice. The embers smolder all year until finally igniting on the solstice.

Atheraels are curious, secretive, and charismatic. Though they may keep a part of themselves in the shadows, they are known for being bright and charming. Highly adaptable and well-spoken, they could enjoy talking to a rock and be charming enough for the rock to reply. They love learning new things and many are taken by their sharp wit, but be warned that an Atherael's personality can be as unpredictable as an unattended bonfire.

TODAY'S HOROSCOPE:

Take a deep breath. Okay, cool. Take another one. This is gonna be hard, but you're going to let other people talk today, and you're going to listen. I don't know why. Either you've been talking too much or, like, you need to take a break from trying to help because something is gonna happen. Like, something important.

Go eat something really yummy. Yummy things are good. Unless it's not yummy. And if it's not yummy, ew, no, what are you doing, spit it out, don't eat that.

You should also try hazelnut spread on waffles.

That's not actually part of the horoscope. I just think it's really tasty.

YERONE

(JUNE 21 – JULY 22)

This constellation is so named for Yeris and the wave he summons to put out the fire from the summer solstice before it consumes Zebulon. There was once a bonfire so great that he had to summon half the oceans from Aeon to put it out, and some Sages believe shooting stars are him splashing Etheril and Xarapharos's embers to keep them from catching flame before the next solstice.

Yerones are passionate, protective, and sensitive. Their emotions are as vast as the ocean and are often hidden behind many walls. Feeling so much can make them moody and cranky, but they are also capable of great creativity and love. Earning their trust is a gift, and while a Yerone may forgive you for breaking it, they will not forget. They're more likely to conveniently forget how to swim if you ever need to be saved from drowning.

TODAY'S HOROSCOPE:

Today is the day we get creative! You're going to take all that awesome energy and brain thinking stuff, and you're gonna make something cool with it. Never done art before? No problem! Just grab a pen or a brush or anything at all and put your thought bits down on paper or cardboard or something. When you're done, hang it up so you can admire it because what? You're super amazing, and you can do anything!

Watch out for grumpy people. Yes, you may care about them, but today is the day you give them space and don't bother them. Focus on you.

~~Hmm... I know a grumpy person...~~

Whatever. I love youuuuu! **Shut up.** Love you too.

MONDELO

(JULY 23 – AUGUST 22)

So named for Mondet, the proud and powerful Asran warrior who was the first king of Xenon. Great Azaethoth honored his brave victory by casting his image in the stars so that no one, mortal or god, could ever forget Mondet's Rebellion.

Mondelos are creative, passionate, and radiant. They are natural leaders who shine like stars under pressure and enjoy showing off their talents. They are romantic, loyal, and often vain. Though their confidence may manifest as arrogance, they are known for their very big hearts and can be quite sensitive. Don't ever insult a Mondelo unless you want them to raise an army and come after you. Hint: You will not win.

TODAY'S HOROSCOPE:

You already know that today is gonna be fifty flavors of awesome because the world has the pleasure of having you in it! You're gonna have the most super day ever, and I hope you take lots of time for you. Family is gonna wear you out super hard, but you love them lots. I know they're crazy, but things are really gonna get better. I swear. Maybe. Unless they don't. And then I'm sorry.

Keep working on the project thing you've got going. Don't listen to the hater people because they're big meanies. You don't need that kind of icky energy in your life, and they're not worth a second glance.

Remember that being so super cool can be exhausting, so don't forget to take a nap.

Naps are awesome.

ERNKAEL

(AUGUST 23 – SEPTEMBER 22)

Sages say these stars honor Merikath, who after completing the feast for Merikatha always falls asleep before joining in the meal. She is said to spend weeks preparing and by the time it's all done, she's too exhausted to eat. They believe she dozes off too close to the ledges in Zebulon and often falls off, creating craters in the moon when she lands.

Ernkaels are meticulous, organized, and kind. They're hard workers who don't mind taking on big jobs, and their natural ability to organize and quick minds make fast work of any task. They love little details, which makes them very thorough and quite picky. Ernkaels seek total perfection and though they are caring, they can be obsessive and harsh. Be careful aggravating them. They may make a crater just to put you in one.

Today's Horoscope:

It's time to let that sock go. The one you've been waiting for the other sock, its socky mate, to return? I don't know how to tell you this, and I hate that it's gotta be me, but it's not coming back. You have to say goodbye. Make it into a cool puppet or, like, use it to hold beans or something.

You could buy more socks or just wear a different sock with it. They won't match, you know, but the sock could go on being a sock instead of wasting away in your laundry basket or up on one of those cutesy clippy things people put lonely socks on.

Drink something sweet today.

Not because I predicted it, but just because I think it would a nice way to treat yourself after you get rid of the sock.

BRAEL

(SEPTEMBER 23 – OCTOBER 22)

These stars are so named for the sacred bridge of Xenon, the world that connects Aeon to Zebulon. Before the Asra ruled Xenon, Babbeth would walk the bridge on his way to break the veil between worlds to allow souls of the dead to pass through for Dhankes. After the gods were forbidden from entering Xenon, Great Azaethoth made a bridge of stars in the sky for Babbeth to walk once more.

Braels are charming, sociable, and diplomatic. They fall in love or lust quickly, and they adore beauty and the finer things in life. They are known for being fair and clever enough to usually avoid conflict, though their desire for peace can make them indecisive. They are top-notch negotiators and mediators, but just don't ask a Brael what they want to eat for dinner. They will not be able to choose. Choose for them.

TODAY'S HOROSCOPE:

I know that it's impossible for you to make any kind of decision, Mr. or Mrs. or Miss or Mx. Brael, but you gotta try to make a teeny tiny one today. Now I can't tell you what it is. That would be cheating, but you can do it. I totally believe in you. Use that big brain of yours to figure out what you need to do and just go for it. If you take a few deep breaths and think it over in that super cool diplomatic way you do, you'll see that making a decision is actually the best decision ever.

Don't forget to drink plenty of water.

Do something nice for yourself. Get something shiny or yummy and enjoy it because you're totally amazing.

MOLBROT

(OCTOBER 23 – NOVEMBER 21)

The Sages believe these stars represent the hole in the veil Babbeth creates to allow souls through for Dhankes so they can see their loved ones again. His tentacles wear the veil down until it shatters, and then he must spend several agonizing weeks repairing the damage to close it back up. As long as these stars hang high in the sky, the veil between worlds is thin and communication with the dead and the gods is possible.

Molbrots are powerful, passionate, and intense. They can charm just about anyone, and their dominant personas make them difficult to refuse. The emotional depth that makes Molbrots so intriguing, however, also makes them brooding and stubborn. Once they've made up their mind, they will do everything in their power to get it. Best to stay out of their way when that happens because they care very little about the consequences as long as they get what they want.

TODAY'S HOROSCOPE:

Dear Molbrot, please be nice today. Don't be a Molbrat. Just because you really want that shiny new outfit or that new car doesn't mean you get to be a jerk to people. Take a few deep breaths and remember that you are pretty awesome even without those things. It's okay to actually not get something that you want. I swear. It's super fine. Your head is not going to explode or anything, pinkie promise. Remember that your journey in this life isn't one that you walk alone, and you risk ticking off the people around you when you don't consider their needs too.

Also, try to brood less.

Also also, you look awesome in leather.

Hurnkrone

(November 22 – December 21)

Sages hold Hurnkrone to be the most sacred of all the stars because the home of the gods, Zebulon, is hidden deep within this constellation. This is the time of year that the days grow short and the nights long, and Great Azaethoth visits the world, hidden in the ample shadows as the stars of his crown dim.

Hurnkrones are joyful, bold, and captivating. Though this is the darkest time of the year, they shine like the sun wherever they are. They have equally bright perspectives and tend to be optimistic, and they crave the thrill of new experiences. Being tied down bores them, and they may not always be the most reliable. Good luck getting a Hurnkrone to sit still. Though they're not the most responsible, they're definitely the most fun.

TODAY'S HOROSCOPE:

We both know you want to go do the thing. You know which one I'm talking about. The thing you're really excited about even though you have that other thing already planned for that same day. I know the other thing is boring and you don't wanna, but you gotta. Maybe you promised, maybe people are really depending on you. I dunno. I just know you gotta suck it up and handle it. You can do the really fun thing later, I promise. Think of it like a treat for getting your chores done.

Take some time to look up at the stars tonight.

But whatever you do, do not eat onions today. Please. For the love of all the gods, stay away from onions. I can see it very clearly, and it's just super bad. No onions.

No.

BELTARAEL

(DECEMBER 22 – JANUARY 19)

This group of stars honors the chariot driven by Beltara. After the winter solstice, she takes the stars in Great Azaethoth's crown to the sun one by one to relight them so that the days will grow long again. Even while Great Azaethoth dreams, she makes the journey each year, often using the flames from the fires lit on the winter solstice to hasten her work.

Beltaraels are patient, funny, and responsible. They are focused on doing whatever needs to be done, whether it's at work or home, to be successful. This dedication makes them very dependable, but it also makes it difficult for them to connect because duty takes priority over others' feelings. To bridge the gaps in their people skills, many Beltaraels are blessed with a great sense of humor, so they'll entertain you but still remind you not to buy that new shirt you want.

TODAY'S HOROSCOPE:

Dear Beltarael, you need a break. Okay, we get it. You're as hardworking as Beltara, dragging those stars back and forth across the universe to set them on fire or whatever for Great Azzy. But you need some chill time too. You gotta recharge your natural awesome energy so you can keep on shining like the super star you are.

Read a book, eat yummy treats, get a foot rub if you're into that kinda thing—do whatever you find relaxing!

EXCEPT WORKING.

Working is not relaxing. That is the opposite of relaxing. Don't do that.

Also, beware of left shoes. You might, like, trip or something. The other ones are all right though.

Classifications of Magic

Magic is divided into five schools under Lucian teachings that claim all magical powers originate from the natural world and can be measured within specific elements of earth, air, fire, water, and the divine. Any spiritual connection is attributed to the Lord of Light. Magic users will be registered in one of these five classes if they show signs of having magical ability and pass magical aptitude testing.

Though Sages acknowledge the power of the elements and their role in magical rituals and spells, they believe magic is too diverse to classify in a mere five categories. They instead attribute the various presentations of magical ability to certain gods, and their naming system is designed to honor a specific deity.

As gods are multifaceted beings, it is not unusual for them to have more than one type of magic attributed to them. There are even cases of two contradicting forms of magic, such as restorative and destructive, being assigned to the same god. For example, Baub's Rage is a very powerful form of destructive fire magic, but there is also Baub's Embrace, a type of earth magic that is known for restoring strength and vitality.

Some types of magic that are especially powerful or unique are highly regulated or flat-out illegal. Teleportation requires a special license and licensees are closely monitored by authorities because of the potential for criminal use. Anything that falls under necromancy, including the creation of ghouls, is against the law and punishable by imprisonment. Licenses range from A, B, C, D classes to S class (most highly regulated of all).

Magic requires some sort of object to conjure it. That object can be a wand or other enhanced item, the words of a spell, or a simple gesture depending on the skills of the witch. Being able to use magic with only a thought is generally reserved for gods and the everlasting. The rare few mortals who have no magical ability are registered as voids, and the Sages called them Silenced. Silenced can still use magical objects, but they cannot call on any magic of their own.

DIVINE

The Sages believe people with this magic are touched by starlight, as in they have been blessed directly by Great Azaethoth himself. This magic encompasses abilities from all the other classifications of magic and will often surpass them. Witches of starlight usually develop the natural skill to cast spells without any incantations, which sets them apart from other witches who must speak the words of a spell to cast it. Even with lots of years of practice, very few non-starlight witches can learn to do this.

Starlight witches have another edge to their magic as their spells will almost always be more powerful than any other magic user. The most novice starlight witch could potentially be more powerful than advanced witches in other disciplines. They are inclined to learn advanced forms of magic such as teleportation, telekinesis, and even forbidden arts such as necromancy and blood magic.

Starlight itself is a powerful element as it has huge restorative potential and equally massive destructive properties. The sacred light of stars can heal wounds just as easily as it can cause them, and witches under this discipline have historically been great healers and warriors.

FIRE

Fire is the element of passion, love, strength, and many dangerous forms of destruction magic. It is the one element that can't be touched without harm, but it is also an element of healing as it can be warm, comforting, and create a path for a new life to flourish. It is associated with the south and colors like red and orange. Star signs include Lithone, Mondelo, and Hurnkrone. Sagittarian fire disciplines include but are not limited to:

× Baub's Rage incredibly destructive wildfires

× Shartorath's Hearth gentle fire with healing properties

× Merikath's Embers simmering hot flames, good for cooking

× Galgareth's Flame love and sex magic (formerly Urilith's)

× Beltara's Chariot another destructive form of fire characterized by controlled streams of flame, like the tire tracks of a big car.

Or a chariot...

Ohhhh I get it now.

WATER

Water is the element of healing, purification, emotion, and the mind. It is vital for all life on our planet and is thought to be needed for resurrection spells, though those secrets have been lost to time. Though it is essential to life, it can also be detrimental in excess or in its frozen form. Its ever-changing nature connects it to emotions and dreams. It is associated with the west and the color blue. Star signs include Zitrone, Yerone, and Molbrot. Water disciplines for Sages include but are not limited to:

× Yeris's Tears destructive ice abilities

× Galmelthar's Touch healing and restorative abilities magic

× Salgumel's Slumber dream magic oooOooOooo!

× Merikath's Cauldron mild healing magic, helps with cooking

× Halandrach's Wave destructive weather magic (rains, storms, floods). Common discipline for twins where the other will have Zunnerath's Crest. I dunno what happens when there's triplets. Maybe they just make something up for that. XD

EARTH

Earth is the element of knowledge, stability, strength, and vitality. It is the foundation of all worlds, from Aeon to Zebulon, for even the home of the gods has stone floors. It is known for its vivacious ability to give life to lush forests and fields, but also its harsh cruelty in denying it with desolate places like deserts and icy wastelands. Star signs are Halrael, Ernkael, and Beltarael. It is associated with the north and the colors green and brown. Sagittarian disciplines include but are not limited to:

× Ulgon's Roar destructive earth magic that crushes and quakes

× Zarbaun's Bounty revitalizing magic commonly used with plants

× Baub's Embrace healing magic that helps with strength and vitality

× Babbeth's Touch destructive earth magic that leeches life away

× Bestrath's Hand weak form of earth magic that helps with farming and construction (the idea being that Bestrath helped grow the food for the first Dhankes and built the table for the feast!)

AIR

Air is the element of communication, curiosity, intellect, and the soul. It is the power of things unseen and is as essential to life as other elements. It is connected to souls as air is what carries them between the worlds after death, and it is so vital there is even a breeze that blows through Zebulon, powered by Great Azeathoth's breath as he sleeps. Star signs are Atherael, Brael, and Baubel. It is associated with the east and colors yellow and white. Disciplines for Sages included but are not limited to:

× Baub's Breath destructive air magic

× Meuvothin's Touch mild healing magic granting the witch skills with brewing beer because of the yeast thingies making little bubbles!

× Galmelthar's Whisper healing magic

× Solmach's Hammer magic that is both mildly destructive and healing

× Zunnerath's Crest destructive weather magic (tornados, hurricanes). The other half that complements Halandrach's wave, seen in twins.

GIFTS OF STARSIGHT

Not to be confused with the magical element and power of starlight, the gift of starsight is another rare blessing from Great Azaethoth himself. Though they are his gifts, they're often named after skills known to be possessed by other gods to identify exactly what they do.

× Babbeth's Tongue communication with the dead

× Great Azaethoth's Glimmer seeing the future :D

× Abeth's Lashes read any language ever, including godstongue

× Zarbaun's Kiss ability to communicate with and command plants

× Eyes of Yeris see all that is hidden, arguably the most powerful form of starsight ever (GO ME! :D you know, except for all the trauma)

The Sagittarian Gods

There are literally hundreds of gods. HUNDREDS. I decided to name as many of the super duper important ones as I could, and they're all listed by how they're related to Loch. (Being the most important god ever, it totally makes sense!)

Loch told you to say that, didn't he?

Maaaybe. But it is actually super easy since he's one of the gods we know the best, so he's a good point of referral. If we knew who Rota was, I would do this list based off how he's related to everybody! :D

...Whatever.

Anyway. Right. Hundreds of gods! Most Sages worship Great Azaethoth since he's the big old god in charge of everything, and many also revere a ~~pacific~~ specific pantheon honored with their own sabbaths. Obviously, there are Sages who worship gods who don't have their own days, but the ones with sabbaths are def in the popular kids club:

Galmelthar (Galmethas)

Urilith (Urilitha)

Zarbaun (Zarbeltha)

Meuvothin (Summer Solstice)

Babbeth (Babbas)

Merikath (Merikatha)

Bestrath (Dhankes)

Galgareth (Winter Solstice)

The Gods' Family Tree

Great Azaethoth

Etheril ✦ Xarapharos

Bestrath ✦ Halandrach ✦ Zunnerath ✦ Babbeth ✦ Merikath

Rordanus ✦ Galmethar   Abigail the Starkiller   Urilith ✦ Mevvothin

Zarbaun ✦ Baub   Abeth ✦ Beltara

Stoker

Urilith ✦ Salgumel

Chandralen   Shartaroth ✦ Gordoth ✦ Yeris ✦ Ulgon ✦ Elgrirath ✦

Zarnorach ✦ Xarbon ✦ Solmach ✦ Eb ✦ Ebb

Ebbeth ✦ Lozathin

Tollmathar ✦ Gronoch ✦ Xhorlas   Sloane Beaumont

✦ Galgareth ✦ Azaethoth

Pandora

ABETH THE ERUDITE
GODDESS OF THE WRITTEN WORD AND LIBRARIES

Beltara's twin, Child of Abigail and Zunnerath, Stoker's sis

Rides around with Beltara and their grand-niece Chandraleth on the aurora borealis doin' cool goddess stuff

AZAETHOTH THE LESSER
GOD OF TRICKERS, THIEVES, AND DIVINE RETRIBUTION

Loch! :D

BABBETH THE SAGACIOUS
GOD OF DEATH, FUNERALS, AND LOST CHILDREN

Gave Sloane an old gold coin as a wedding present. Creepy. His orchard has special fruit and bees and stuff for sacred noms.

Babbas is his day!

BAUB THE PURE
GOD OF WAR, DIVINE WRATH, AND ORGANIZATION

Loch's grandpa! Responsible for the Sweep of Zebulon where he went all crazy and cleaned everything and made like a big meteor shower or something :D

Spawn of Zunnerath and Halandrach

AZAETHOTH THE LESSER

BELTARA THE FACE
GODDESS OF INSOMNIA, LOST THINGS, AND FALLING STARS

Loch's cousin, twice removed. Daughter of Zunnerath and Abigail the Starkiller, Abeth's twin, Stoker's big sis!

Her unusual naming comes from Great Azaethoth saying he saw himself when he looked at her, so she was named 'Face' for the vision of Great Azaethoth her greatness inspired.

BESTRATH THE BENEVOLENT
GOD OF THE HARVEST AND TURNING OF THE SEASONS

Loch's great-granduncle, and his day is Dhankes

CHANDRALETH THE BRILLIANT
GODDESS OF NAPS, FRIENDSHIP, AND EVISCERATION

Loch's half-sister, directly spawned by Salgumel after carrying her around inside him for a hundred years :D

CLEUS THE FANCIFUL
GOD OF PAGEANTRY, DISSECTION, AND REGENERATION

Loch's third cousin, twice removed, on his mother's side

Deceased X_X

EB THE FIRST
GOD OF STRIFE AND PANIC

Loch's uncle! Him and his bro Ebb and Ebbeth were spawned directly from Baub's boob with a mere thought. The triplets are said to be born from the horrors of war Baub endured in battle and their combined powers create and fuel nightmares.

EBB THE SECOND
GOD OF DISCORD AND FEAR

Also Loch's uncle!

EBBETH THE LAST
GOD OF DISSENSION AND TERROR

Also also Loch's uncle!

ELGRIRATH THE ASTUTE
GODDESS OF REGRET, WIT, AND MISSED OPPORTUNITIES

Loch's aunt!

ETHERIL
GOD OF MIST AND LIGHT

Loch's great-great-grandpa

GALGARETH THE BELOVED

GALGARETH THE BELOVED
GODDESS OF SERENDIPITY, NIGHT, AND LOVE

Loch's sister :D

Winter solstice is her day

GALMELTHAR THE WANDERER
GOD OF KINDNESS, BOREDOM, AND MERCY

Galmethas is his day, Urilith's ex-hubby

Loch's cousin, twice removed

(the Slut!)
GORDOTH ~~THE UNTOUCHED~~
GOD OF JUSTICE AND RIGHTEOUS WRATH

Loch's uncle!

GORDOTH THE UNTOUCHED

GREAT AZAETHOTH
GOD OF CREATION AND FATHER OF ALL

Loch's great-great-great-grandfather and creator of everything ever that has ever freakin' been

GRONOCH THE BRIGHT
GOD OF HEALING AND ATTRITION

Loch's brother, deceased X_X

HALANDRACH
GODDESS OF SKIES, CLOUDS, AND THE RAIN

Killed by Abigail the Starkiller D:

Loch's great-grandma, deceased X_X

KINDRESS
GOD OF LIFE AND DEATH, THE CHAOS OF THE INTERSTICE

Great Azaethoth's firstborn, bad news bears all around

Would be Loch's great-great-granduncle if he's real :D

GREAT AZAETHOTH

LOZATHIN THE DELICATE
GOD OF WAR AND FAMINE

Loch's uncle!

MERIKATH THE FAMISHED
GODDESS OF COOKING AND GLUTTONY

Loch's great-grandaunt, spawned Urilith and Meuvothin

Merikatha is her day! :D nom nom nommm

MEUVOTHIN THE ASTRAL
GODDESS OF SUNLIGHT, FERMENTATION, AND CRIMSON

Loch's aunt (but also like his cousin? ^^;;)

Is responsible for giving the gift of beermaking to mortals!

Summer solstice is her day! :D :D :D WITH LOTS OF BEER!

RORDANUS THE PERSPICACIOUS
GOD OF DYING BREATHS, AGONAL GASPS, AND NEEDLEPOINT

Loch's cousin, twice removed, consort of Babbeth

SALGUMEL THE UNFAILING

Salgumel the Unfailing
God of Dreams and Sleep

Has gone crazy in his dreaming as all the cults who have tried to wake him up have gone mad, and it's pretty well known that he'll destroy the world if he gets up from his napnap

Loch's father :D

Shartorath the Willful
Goddess of Marriage and the Home

Loch's aunt

Solmach the Fierce
Goddess of Blacksmith, Metalworking, and Cheese

Loch's aunt!

Tollmathan the Seeker
God of Poetry and Plagues

Loch's oldest brother, deceased X_X

Ulgon the Valiant
Goddess of Wisdom, Horses, and the Hunt

Loch's aunt!

URILITH THE BENIGNANT

URILITH THE BENIGNANT
GODDESS OF FERTILITY, PREGNANCIES, AND ~~LOVE~~

Loch's mommy! :D I think she gave up being a love goddess after her divorce, but Idk for sure. I dun wanna ask her. :D

Urilitha is her day! :D

XARAPHAROS
GOD OF DARKNESS AND FOG

Loch's great-great-grandpa

XARBON THE FAIR
GOD OF VANITY, MANICURES, AND HOSPITALITY

Loch's uncle!

XHORLAS THE CLEMENT
GOD OF PASSION AND CHARMS

Loch's brother (alive... for now :D)

YERIS THE CAPRICIOUS
GOD OF THE OCEAN AND HIDDEN THINGS

Loch's uncle!

ZARBAUN THE LAVISH
GOD OF BEAUTY AND FLORA

Zarbeltha is their day! Spawned by
Halandrach, so Baub's half-brother and
Loch's great-granduncle

ZARNORACH THE OBSTINATE
GODDESS OF PERTINACITY, VICTORY, AND SHOES

Loch's aunt

ZUNNERATH
GOD OF STONE, MOUNTAINS, AND THE WINDS

Loch's great-grandpa

The Everlasting Races

THE ASRA

Giant feline beasts who rule over Xenon and possess the ability to shapeshift and create portals in and between worlds. They also have very potent sleeping spells and cannot be silenced. Created by Great Azaethoth to serve the old gods until they rebelled and won their freedom.

Like most of the everlasting, they do not need to speak spells to cast or to use their natural gifts.

Wear beads on their ear tentacles to communicate marital status, special life events, and other information to fellow Asra—including preferred pronouns, as the Asra are an intersex species and will choose to present as either he, she, or they.

Asran culture can be fickle and outright contradictory. They like riddles and puzzles, and wit is a highly prized trait for their kind.

They live the longest of the everlasting races, up to thousands of years, and they have unique funeral rites that allow for an elder to "die" while they're still technically alive. They will have a funeral and entomb them, after which the "deceased" slips into a dreaming similar to the gods. It may take centuries for them to naturally pass on this way.

When they still lived on Aeon, their graves were at risk of being raided because of the magical properties of their bones. They were sought for shapeshifting, portals,

ASRA

and astral projection. The royal family is charged with entombing and watching over the dead, especially as many of them are not technically dead and quite vulnerable.

Beware if a member of the royal family asks for assistance entombing a body. You will end up engaged according to a little-known tradition that states only the royal family take on the responsibility of protecting the dead. Asking to share that duty is the same as asking to be a member of the royal family.

THE VULGORA

Large fish worms known for their fertility and complicated clan system.

It is said that there is still a population of Vulgora who live deep within the Mariana Trench, but it has never been confirmed.

They love arranged marriages, complex politics, and their bite is quite venomous. Their big scales are prized for protection spells, though hunting was not common as they shed them regularly and could easily be scavenged. It is said that the Vulgora would barter their own scales with early mortals before they had to flee Aeon.

Part of what makes the Vulgora's fertility so legendary is that even males of their species can get pregnant and carry young. Both male and female Vulgora produce eggs inside a special pouch deep in their bodies, and any introduction of sperm from a male can fertilize them. They carry the eggs for three months before they hatch and are birthed live.

Although mature Vulgora can survive in and out of water, their young must be born in water and remain there for the first year of life before their lungs are developed enough to breathe air. They are born in large pods of ten to twelve, and most families will have marriage contracts ready for their spawn while they're still eggs.

They live in small clans ruled over by the elder members

Vulgora

of the family who are in charge of all major decisions, especially when matters of marriage are concerned. There is a major focus on wealth and power, and the elders will always pick a marriage to a cruel family who has riches rather than a kind family who has nothing.

THE DEVARACH

They are small goblins with slimy skin, big heads, and thick manes of tentacles.

They believe in communal property and take things at will since everything belongs to everyone, and whoever needs something the most will get it. They prefer to live underground in burrows or dens in large communities made of many families, and they work together and share resources. They could once be found all over the world, but seemed to like the heat of jungles and deserts most of all.

Their skin is slimy because of a natural mucus they produce. Suited for hot climates, they can absorb water molecules from the very air around them through their skin, and it helps them hold in moisture so they don't dehydrate. When a Devarach is scared or in pain, their skin will release a deadly toxin that seeps into the mucus. Anyone who touches them will be poisoned, though other Devarach are naturally immune.

It is rumored that the mucus has magical healing properties, but no one has been able to cultivate it successfully—if the Devarach have, they've not said.

The Devarach focus on the needs of the many and their familial group is put above all else. However, this is not to say that there is no individual attention—after all, a person can best help their family if they're happy, and so the

DEVARACH

Devarach have a strong system for health care, including required periods of rest and relaxation to help treat mental health as well.

As personal happiness is important, marrying for love is encouraged. A happy couple will better serve the community than one that is miserable.

THE ELDRESS

They are a race of horned equine creatures who appear to be actively decomposing. Their horns can range from one to a dozen or more, and they have no skin. *(zombie unicorns!)*

They once ate their dead as a sign of respect and to honor their passing, but now they perform embalming to discourage it. Because they're said to be somewhere between life and death, alive but rotting, Eldress have the ability to communicate through the veil between worlds. An Eldress on Aeon could speak to an Eldress on Xenon, for example. This power is limited to their own kind, although it is rumored some Eldress can speak to the dead regardless of race.

Their milky eyes produce a thick substance known as Eldress tears that is highly poisonous, and it is not advised to follow a fleeing Eldress—they run so fast that their eyes will water, and their tears may fly back and accidentally poison whoever is behind them. Their horns are prized for their hallucinogenic properties and are believed to give visions and heal all wounds, but it is more likely that people who consume the horns are merely high.

Although their teeth are long and thin like needles and may appear fragile, they are more than capable of biting through bone. Their lower jaw can unhinge much in the same way as a snake's so that they can eat things much larger than themselves.

ELDRESS

They're very social creatures and live in large familial groups. It is not uncommon to mate in threes or fours, and these polyamorous units will live together and raise their children.

THE FAEDRA

They are giants with loose pale skin that hangs from their bones in thick folds and have small gossamer wings that allow them to fly for short distances. They don't have eyes or noses, but they do have big mouths full of large sharp teeth.

When they lived on Aeon, the Faedra dwelled in the forests and looked after the trees and plants. When it rained, their bodies would absorb it and swell up like giant balloons. They'd then store and use the water to care for their gardens, their bodies deflating as the water was depleted.

Faedra are solitary creatures whose sole focus is to create and maintain beautiful gardens. They do marry, but even the most affectionate couples will still live in their own separate gardens. When expecting a child, they create a brand-new garden and live there until the child is old enough to be on their own. They will then leave the child to live in the garden they made for them and return to their own.

The Faedra are peaceful creatures with a culture limited to their love of plants. They do not sing, they do not dance, and they do not even write as they have no written language. They communicate only in whispers because they believe loud noises upset their plants. They do not eat any meat or animal product, choosing to survive off the fruits and nuts that they get from their gardens.

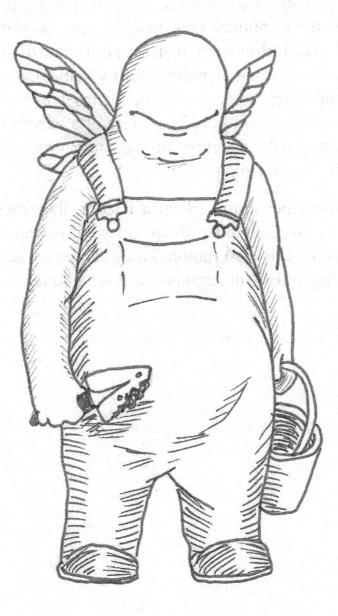

FAEDRA

Although they are a gentle race, they are fiercely protective of both their children and gardens. Any person foolish enough to disturb either will face the full wrath of a Faedra's power, which is the incredible ability to manipulate space and time. Trespassers will find themselves aging fifty years or more in a blink. The edges of a Faedra's garden are marked with skeletons of previous intruders that are left there as a warning.

If someone needs to call on a Faedra, they must bring a new seedling or plant as an offering and apology for trespassing. It is also rumored they can be appeased with gardening tools, wind chimes, or peanut butter.

The Absola

They are large trolls with thick tusks that protrude from their lower jaw. They have long tails, and their skin can be many colors, though shades of green and blue are most common. Purple is most rare and considered lucky as this is the color associated with Great Azaethoth.

The tusks develop when they're adolescents and gift them with psychic communication. If their tusks are removed or broken, the ability will be lost. The tusks can grow back, but it will take many years. They have a system of hand signals similar to human sign language to communicate when this occurs as the tusks can make speaking difficult.

They are a very passionate race who love to spar and dance, and tusk loss is not unusual. The tusks tend to break low and rarely break again below a point that has already been broken as they grow back stronger and thicker than before. This results in their tusks having multiple rings that show how many times they have been damaged. Absola with lots of rings are considered to be especially attractive as it's inferred that they are very active and experienced.

The Absola have very elaborate courting rituals, and both must receive their potential mate's family's blessing before they can wed. This will be achieved by each Absola's family hosting a festival for the other to show off their dancing and fighting abilities. As the females are usually bigger than males, they focus on battle skills while the smaller and leaner males are known for their extremely

ABSOLA

acrobatic dancing. A sign of a successful wedding night is for the new couple to break at least one tusk.

Their other standard of beauty is based on the girth of their tails. A thick tail is considered very attractive for either sex, and many wear jewelry around them to draw attention there. Some Absola wear padded bands to make their tails appear thicker than they actually are, though this practice is looked down upon.

THE MOSTAISTLIS

The Mostaistlis are deformed humanoid creatures with hunched backs and black skin. They are known for painting elaborate designs all over their bodies in white paint and having impressive night vision.

Their paint, called bildena, can take hours or even days to apply. Total perfection must be achieved, and they love symmetrical designs with intricate details. Certain patterns have special meanings amongst their people, but they do not share this information with outsiders.

Their hunched backs are caused by years of bending over to put on their bildena and crawling around small cave passages, though this is of little concern to them as they are a sedimentary people. They once lived in limestone caves where they could mine chalk to mix for their paint, and they rarely traveled outside as they can live for weeks off a single meal.

That single meal is ambrosia, a magically brewed nutritious beverage that is of the utmost importance to the Mostaistlis and vital for their survival. It is very high in alcohol content but has little to no effect on them no matter how much they drink as they process alcohol differently than other races.

The recipe for ambrosia is a secret, as much of the Mostaistlis culture is, but it is known that making it is extremely time-consuming. They had to travel great

Mostaistlis

distances for the ingredients, the brewing process goes on for months, and must be done in complete darkness. This is yet another reason they are not a particularly active people, as they will sit around for weeks at a time to oversee the fermentation.

Multiple families work and live together to make the ambrosia, creating entire colonies within large cave systems. If they need more room, they simply dig more caves. A common Mostaistlis method of proposing is to dig a hole and show it to their perspective mate, a reflection of when their people still lived underground and a new cave would mean the start of a new family.

MORTALS

They were the last of Great Azaethoth's creations and were once called Kronan in honor of the Hurnkrone constellation that was said to be high in the sky when the first man walked Aeon. Kronan was also the original name for Sages before Lucian intervention.

Because of Great Azaethoth's miserable cycle of grief with his firstborn child, the Kindress, he decided that no creature should have the power of resurrection—however, he made an exception for mortals as they have the shortest lifespan of his creations and are quite fragile by comparison.

That's it?

That's all there is to say about humans?!

I mean, I guess we're really not that cool. We don't have fur or cool claws or anything. No wings, no tails, and no tentacles at all! We're so super squishy! :D :D :D

Oh! We have opposable thumbs though! Those are rad. A few humans are double-jointed and can do that weird quick eye wiggle thing like that one dude in that movie. Some of us can curl our tongues and wiggle our ears...

Huh.

MORTAL

Can Asra wiggle their ears like people do?
Can Faedra curl their tongues!? Can an
Eldress juggle!? O: O: O:

Oleander Logue, asking the important questions.

When I find out, I'm not gonna tell you so
ha! >:D

The Sabbaths

GALMETHAS

FEBRUARY 1ST

Galmethas is a holiday of cleaning, purification, and the coming of spring. It is said that the gods decided not to clean their home one winter after the solstice celebration because they would much rather sleep until the warm weather returned. Baub was enraged by the mess and crafted a broom out of a meteor shower to tidy up with, and his sweeping was so powerful that it threatened to destroy Zebulon. In order to calm him, Galmelthar brewed a lemon beer and told him it was for a spiritual cleanse. Baub drank until he passed out and thus started an ancient tradition that is carried on to this very day.

Sages use this time to acknowledge that spring will be returning soon, and they perform many rituals to cleanse their body, mind, and homes. Special baths are prepared, lemon beer is brewed, and several types of cleaning solutions are mixed using a lemon powder that was made at the previous year's Merikatha. As Galmelthar is a god of kindness, Sages can honor him by using this holiday to plan good deeds to perform in the coming months. He is also the god of boredom, so playing games, making crafts, engaging in sexual activity, and planning trips for the coming year are common as well.

URILITHA

MARCH 21ST

Urilitha hails the return of spring and a time to celebrate fertility. This was once a very sexually charged holiday when gods would openly mate with mortals and the everlasting people alike, though it is tamer now that the gods are in the dreaming. The union of Galmelthar and Urilith would signal the start of the celebrations, though other gods took over this duty when they divorced. It ends when the sun rises the following morning, but some gods have been known to keep the festivities going for weeks.

Though the sexual aspect is no longer performed in modern times, Sages still sing and dance, play drums, feast, and they decorate eggs and make fertility totems. The eggs honor the old gods as many of them lay eggs to reproduce, and the eggs are painted and covered with magical signs to represent something the Sage wants to manifest for the coming year. The egg is then planted as a symbol of a witch's intent to hopefully grow that wish to fruition. Fertility totems are long garlands woven out of flowers and vines to represent the twisted tentacles of the gods in coitus. Prayers to Urilith are chanted as the garland is braided, and then it is hung over a bed for couples hoping to have a child.

ZARBELTHA

MAY 1ST

Zarbeltha celebrates the beauty of nature, the coming of summer, and is a minor fertility holiday. Sages would honor this time of year by making crowns of flowers, planting crops, brewing beer, and preparing herbal briquettes to burn on the summer solstice. Gathering and preparing the herbs for the briquettes was done wearing nothing but flowers. Once the bricks were formed and laid down to dry, revelers would then lay each other down to copulate.

Though the orgies and nudity are no more, modern witches still gather flowers and herbs to make crowns and briquettes, and some brew beer for the coming summer solstice. Another surviving tradition is weaving fertility totems in Zarbaun's honor. To appeal to their vanity, the totems are made with their favorite flowers, hawthorn and violets, and woven to emulate their braided tentacles while praying to them. Instead of hanging the garlands over the bed like those made for Urilith, witches will wear the braided flowers when they go to bed.

Summer Solstice

June 21st

The summer solstice honors the light in the world, the glory of summer, and is also known as Meuvothin's Day. Just before sunrise, a bonfire is lit using the briquettes prepared on Zarbeltha. Etheril and Xarapharos are honored because they built the fire for the first summer solstice, but the most revered deity on this day is Meuvothin. Not only is she goddess of the sun, but she introduced beer one fateful solstice thousands of years ago. Witches wear her color, crimson, to honor her, and drink the beer made during Zarbeltha as it should now be ready.

Contemporary witches may be just as happy to purchase beer or other spirits from the store instead of brewing their own, and they may burn herbal incense sticks or small bricks as opposed to full briquettes. Due to the restrictions of urban living, many Sages may not be able to light big fires and opt to use candles to represent this holiday's traditional flame. Regardless of size, any leftover ashes are saved to make into amulets for protection. The ashes are mixed into red clay, molded into solar shapes like circles and sunbursts, and then they're left in the sun to bake and receive Meuvothin's blessing. If red clay is not available, it is acceptable to paint the amulets red once they're dry.

BABBAS

AUGUST 1ST

Babbas honors the first harvest of grain for the year and baking bread. The grain is cut at sunrise and the first loaves of bread will be baked by the time night has fallen. Bread is significant not only for being a food staple for ancient people, but also because it is an offering for Babbeth. Babbas marks the beginning of his long journey across the sky to break the veil in time for Dhankes, and Sages leave him loaves of bread to take with him. As with the grain harvest, it is a time to reap what's been sown over the year, including reflecting on the manifestations planted during Urilitha.

Modern Sages may not limit themselves to bread and instead bake all manner of cakes and pastries to celebrate this day. It is still expected to leave something out for Babbeth's journey, and parents will often take a "bite" to show little witches that Babbeth has come by their home. Sages who tend gardens use this holiday to harvest and bundle herbs to hang in their homes to dry. Sages who lack green thumbs may do the same with wildflowers and herbs purchased from a store. A feast with lots of bread is common.

MERIKATHA

SEPTEMBER 21ST

The autumn equinox is Merikath's day, and it is celebrated with a grand feast. Sages enjoy the fruits of their labor over the past year and gather together as the gods do for a magnificent meal. Merikath has spent the entire year preparing and is so exhausted that she falls asleep before she gets to take her seat at the table. To show gratitude for Merikath's effort, Sages will prepare a plate for her so she can eat whenever she awakens. It is said that the last thing Merikath does for every meal is pick lemons for lemonade, so a glass of lemonade is an essential Merikatha beverage for guests and as an offering.

For modern Sages, this is a day to feast and share a meal with family and friends. Lemons are picked or bought at the store to make lemonade, and a lemon powder is made from drying out the rinds that will be used next year for the lemon beer and purification potions of Galmethas. Should a guest fall asleep after eating but before helping clean, they are given a crown of lemon peels, deemed Merikath for the day, and must wash all the dishes left over from the meal.

DHANKES

OCTOBER 31ST

Dhankes is another harvest celebration where thanks are given to the gods for a bountiful year. Bestrath hosts a feast for the gods as Merikath may still be sleeping, and Babbeth completes his journey to shatter the veil between worlds so communication with the dead is possible. Sages pray to their deceased loved ones and believe their spirits can hear them and may come visit on this special day. To ensure their loved ones return safely, a candle is lit in a doorway facing west to lead them back to Zebulon.

Many of the ancient traditions are still observed by modern Sages. They feast, leave out offerings for the gods, and believe they can contact their deceased loved ones. A candle will still be lit in a western-facing door, though a window works just as well, and it must be lit by midnight or souls risk being lost on Aeon until the next Dhankes. Babbeth's repair of the veil can be slowed by offering him rich vanilla-flavored food and drink, giving souls more chances to return if their families were unable to light a candle for them.

WINTER SOLSTICE

DECEMBER 21ST

The winter solstice is the longest night of the year, and Sages gather to burn bonfires to shine through the darkness caused by the stars in Great Azaethoth's crown fizzling out in the cold. Food could be scarce this time of year, and families and loved ones would share what they had to enjoy a humble feast together. It is Galgareth's night to walk Aeon, and she lights a fire at dusk for Beltara to reignite Great Azaethoth's stars in his crown. Before Galgareth was born, Beltara had to travel all the way to the sun each time. Galgareth then visits every solstice fire to give her blessing.

Both ancient and modern Sages view this holiday as a time to celebrate family and show appreciation to the gods. Solstice fires shrunk over the years, and many Sages use fireplaces or light candles instead. Evergreen trees and bushes are used as decorations, a promise of the green that will return again in the spring. The exchange of gifts came about from Sages leaving offerings out to thank Galgareth for hastening Beltara's journey only to have them politely declined. Galgareth encouraged Sages to keep the offerings and share them with one another instead.

Ollie's Grimoire :D

Okay so grimoires are a big deal for Sages. We do not have a singular written special thing like the Lucians do with their Litany. Our traditions and beliefs have been passed down generation after generation through oral story time and grimoires, collections of spells and rituals put together by families. No family's grimoire is quite like another, each as unique as the family who owns it.

Since my family is mostly Lucian, I learned about Sage things from the internet (shoutout to the Select Sagittarian, a video series by Scout Bang that was a huge helpppp) and then my starsight showed me all kinds of nifty Sage stuff too.

This is my grimoire, my collection of spells, rituals, and everything that I know about being a Sage plus lots of things I've doodled here and there.

(Special thanks to Professor Emil Kunst for giving me some of his fancy professor things to put in here so I sound smart. You rock, glowy ball dude!)

A BRIEF HISTORY OF THE SAGES

FROM THE NOTES OF PROFESSOR EMIL KUNST

The old gods descended from between the stars of the Hurnkrone constellation, and their worship was structured around the seasons and the movements of celestial bodies. For thousands of years, the old gods and the people of the everlasting races lived with mortals in blissful harmony. This, however, was not to last.

The Lord of Light appeared, calling on mortals to hear his word and acknowledge him as the one true supreme being. After delivering his Litany and mysteriously vanishing, mortals flocked by the hundreds of thousands to worship him. The old gods lost many of their followers, and this massive loss of devotion is what caused Great Azaethoth to go into the dreaming. The other gods followed him, and the old ways began to fade.

The Lucian religion soon dominated the planet, and the faith of the old gods was labeled as blasphemous and unholy. Many were forced to convert or face dire consequences. The magical people of the everlasting races who did not go into the dreaming or flee to Xenon were killed for being abominations in the eyes of the Lord of Light. Within a generation, the Lucian faith decimated the peaceful Sages.

Sages carry on the name to this day, and many see it as a testament to their devout faith. There is a popular idiom amongst worshippers that says changing the name of a star doesn't diminish its shine. Lucians tried to label the old ways and steal them away, but their attempts did nothing to sway the devotion Sages hold for the gods.

"Great Azaethoth has always been, always was, and will always be."

— *Sagittarian proverb*

Sages worship the old gods who are said to be sleeping in the dreaming, a state of deep slumber, up in the city of Zebulon. It's hidden in the stars of the Sagittarius constellation, a special realm connected to the mortal world of Aeon by the world of Xenon. Xenon is the bridge, a special world where all souls must pass through before finding their eternal peace in Zebulon.

It is said that Silenced souls must walk the bridge of Xenon for a hundred years to gain enough of a magical spark to pass over to Zebulon. Their steps power the light of the bridge that helps draw souls there from the other side. No living god is allowed to set foot here since the Asra defeated the gods and were given ~~severity~~ over it. S o v e r eignt y

Since the gods went into the dreaming, Xenon became home to peeps of the everlasting races who fled Aeon to escape being hunted by Lucian jerkwads. It was thought that they were totally extinct and were gone from Aeon. We know now that some of the everlasting peeps were able to survive on Aeon after intermingling with humans, but they live in secret to avoid detection.

The Lucians revere the Lord of Light, the one true god who delivered the Litany of Light 1500 years ago and then like vanished. Claimed to have performed a bunch of miracles and was supposed to get another Litany for people to read but uhhh he never showed back up. Lucians remain faithful, waiting for him to return.

Godstongue is the language of magic created by the old gods. There are versions specific to certain deities that can only be read by the god it was written for or their most devoted followers. Lucians claim this language was given to mankind by the Lord of Light, and there is a Lucian version used for their worship.

Sages generally consider the Lucian version to be obscene and the magic brought on by Lucian spells is said to not be as potent as true godstongue.

Xenish Sprigs are trees that glow white and have strange magical properties including disruption of portal energy. They are native to Xenon where there are whole forests of them, but they will appear when there's been a tear in the veils between worlds.

Starlupen are magical bioluminescent eels that hail from the waters of Xenon. It's said a starlupa can travel through all the worlds from Aeon to Zebulon in the space of a mortal thought by using nothing but moonlight.

Xenon is said to have all kinds of fascinating flora and fauna, but these are the only examples known to peeps on Aeon.

Herbs, Plants, and Stone Things

Burning lavender honors Shartorath and soothes marital troubles. It's used for lots of baby rituals too. Also it just smells super good.

Lemons are super good for cleansing and purification spells, also smell super good.

Amber is sacred to Yeris, and people wear amber charms for good fishing. Well, good for the fisherman, not the fish. Also, just smells like a rock.

Leaving jasmine under your pillow is supposed to bring good dreams from Salgumel. Which makes no sense because he's, like, crazy, so how can he give anyone good dreams right now?

Holly is a common winter solstice planty, and hanging it inside your home is supposed to bring luck all year round. Do not eat them. No matter how tempting the lil' red berries are, they are major yuck town and toxic.

While Zarbaun is said to prefer hawthorn and violets for their offerings, Urilith isn't as picky. She just really loves flowers. She will even accept paper flowers from children who pray to her.

The source of Babbeth's love of vanilla is unknown, but you can totally use vanilla bean to ward off death and sickness. It might at least give you a good head start or somethin'.

Azaethoth the Lesser really likes blue raspberry lollipops.

Rituals

Sagittarian rituals are traditionally performed after the space has been cleansed and a circle is cast. This is not totes necessary for every ritual ever, but it is suggested to keep negative juju out of your magical workings. You don't wanna eat at a dirty table, right? :D

Funerals involve bathing and shrouding the dead person's body before burial. No embalming is done. That's a no-no. A celebration of life follows the burial and can last days or weeks (usually until a new moon at least).

At the other far end of the life spectrum thing, there are welcome or birthing rituals that are performed for newborn Sages. A similar version is performed for the newly converted because they're kinda like little baby Sages too! :D

All the elements are called on to cleanse the space, and the ritual welcomes the new peep into the world and asks them to be a good witch and be kind to others and stuff <333

If the new peep is a baby, then the ritual is directly followed by the naming ritual (more below with the baby stuff).

The new devotee is charged with following the will of the gods even as they slumber, to keep all of the sabbaths sacred, to seek balance in the world and within themselves, and above all else, harm none in what they do.

Neun Monde (literally nine moons) is a big celebration for a new mama- or daddy-to-be. A rich yummy cake is a traditional treat plus lots of other fruits and healthy things PLUSSS all the awesome gifts that the parents will need for the little one's welcome ritual once they're born. It was once a full nine months of worship for the pregnant peep, but it's been kinda scaled back in modern times.

-A bell for the baby's first sound to be music

-Some honey for their first taste to be sweet

-Herbs for their very first smell to be calming

-A blankie so their first touch will be tender

-A crown of lavender so their first sight will be the beauty of their mommy or daddy <3<3<3

"You pass through a ring of fire
to collect your crown of stars."

— *Sagittarian saying about giving birth*

A naming ritual follows the birthing and welcome ceremony, and gods practice a second naming where their title and chosen thingie that they're in charge of is chosen (I am bettering on big fires and lethal cuteness for Panda Bear!)

That's dumb.

Nuh-uh. Pandora is lethally cute. It's true. You're dumb. :D

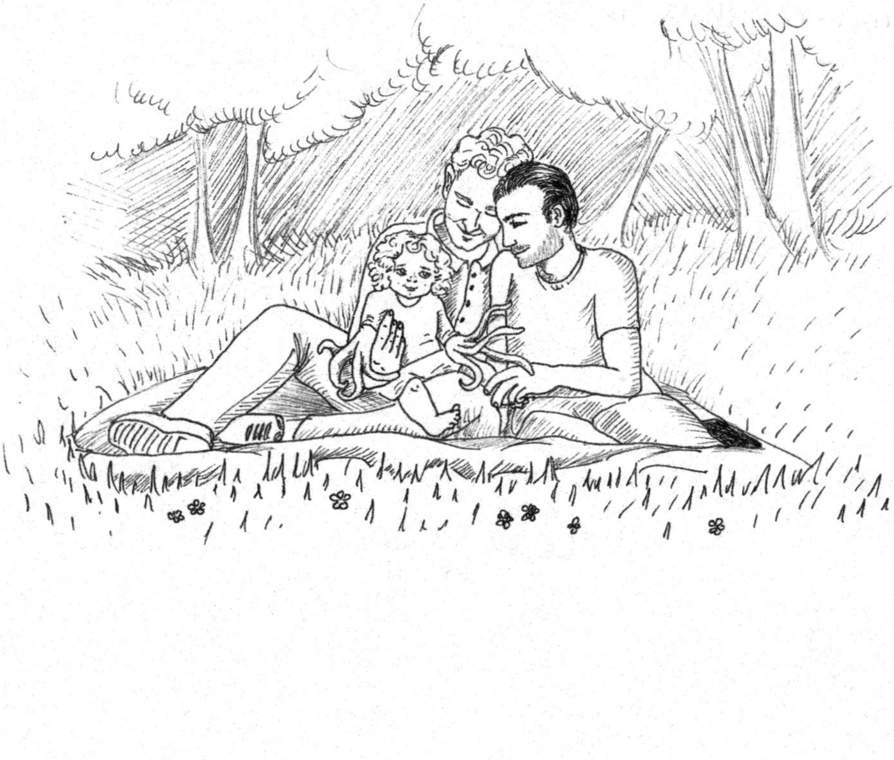

Sages perform handfasting for weddings (Loch insists there were always orgies and big fires, but not sure I believe him).

Weddings traditionally are held under an arch that's built for the ceremony and decorated with flowers. If the wedding is to be inside (which would be, like, super unusual because Sage peeps will get married even in the rain), then a mini arch can be used symbolically.

Purple is a normal color for clothing, flowers, and basically all the wedding décor ever because it's Great Azzy's color.

Wedding rituals invoke blessings of earth for strength, air for joy, water for clarity, fire for passion, and starlight to light the path even in the darkest hours! <3<3<3

And, uh, just FYI...

Sages would totally marry more than one personnnn

hint hint :D :D :D

...whatever.

Ollie's Spells <3<3<3

To Spark Sweet Creativity

This is a special spell I used a lot back when I was having some artsy related issues. I recommend taking this spell in shot form, although you can totally cast a big spell and put it in a glass or pitcher. It totally tastes like that popsicle that's red, white, and blue. You know which one. When your brain is giving you a hard time, cast this spell as needed. :D

1 part blue curacao
1 part raspberry vodka
1 part orange vodka
2 parts sweet and sour mix
Grenadine

Mix the vodkas and sweet and sour mix together and fill up a shot glass halfway. Add a splash of grenadine and let it sink to the bottom. Top off with blue curacao (if you pour slowly down the inside of the shot glass, it should settle on top of the grenadine). The finished shot will have white, blue, and red layers—just like the popsicle!

If not, no worries! I mess it up sometimes and end up with a big blue shot with a red bottom. :D :D :D You can also totally skip the extra pour and mix the blue curacao with the sweet and sour mix and vodkas from the start. The shot won't be as pretty, but it will still be very tasty! :D

Spell to Fix A Grumpy Person

This is a relatively new spell I learned to cast for a certain grumpy person in my life when they're being extra grumpy. One or two casts vastly improves the grumpy mood. Beware of the coconut as this can be a very divisive flavor. It may just agitate your grumpy person more, so please cast with caution.

4 ounces white rum
2 ounces pineapple juice
4 ounces cream of coconut
3 cups of ice

Measure the stuff, put the stuff in the blender, blend stuff, and ta-dah! You've got one super magical spell guaranteed to soften even the grumpiest grumpy bear. Here's a neat trick for measuring if you don't get the mysterious art of ounces – one standard shot glass is usually 1.5 ounces! And hey, if you add a little too much pineapple juice 'cause trying to eyeball half an ounce or whatever in a shot glass is hard, I think it'll still taste pretty good! :D

You can add some fruit to decorate the glass like cherries and pineapple, but that's totally optional. Some people like to add pineapple chunks or a splash of lime to blend with the other stuff. For an extra coconutty punch, you can use coconut rum.

Banish Negative Thoughts

Sometimes you need something bright and happy to cheer yourself up. I highly suggest casting this spell while you watch a super cool movie to chase away any negative juju that might be bothering you. Watch a comedy! Something silly that'll make you laugh! Have a few of these and relax!

2 parts vodka
1 part orange liqueur
1 part lime juice

Mix everything in a shaker with some ice, and shake it well until it's all nice and chilly. Strain into two shot glasses or one big cup. This spell is much more effective with a friend, so I recommend going with two shots so you can share it! Freshly squeezed lime juice is best, but I promise not to judge if you wanna use the stuff that comes in the little plastic lime thing.

No one has to know. Shhhh, I won't tell.

You can also change this spell up by using a flavored vodka instead of the plain stuff. Any citrus type will work, and you can even use pineapple or coconut. Ooo, or vanilla! Vanilla is really good. Oh oh oh or there's that cake-flavored one out now too. Okay, you get the idea. You can try different stuff to find the right spell for you! :D

Sicky Cold Fixer-Upper

This is the absolute best ever spell to cast when you've got the crud. I'm talkin' about the snotty, body ache, creeping variety of crud that gets down into your bones. Casting this spell a few times is sure to knock it out (or at least let you catch some super good snoozes!). Even if you're not sicky, it's a yummy beverage to enjoy when it's chilly and gross outside.

8 parts bourbon whiskey (wild gobble-gobble kind)
16 parts water
3 parts lemon juice
3 parts honey
Nutmeg

Mix the bourbon whiskey, water, and lemon juice together in a heat resistant mug. Heat in the microwave for one minute or in a sauce pan until it simmers. Add honey and a dash of nutmeg, then stir it all together. You can mix in more honey or nutmeg for increased honeyey nutmeggy flavor! Optionally, you can ice this drink and enjoy it cold!

If you wanna be real fancy, you can use fresh nutmeg and grate it right on top. Some people also like to use cloves and cinnamon sticks to give it an extra warm and spicy flavor. If the drinks gets too cool, you can pop it in the microwave to heat it up again! Cast responsibly, kids! :D :D :D

To Rid Thyself of Alkeehol
(A Hangover Potion)

Did you cast a few too many times and forget how to cleanse your body of alcohol? Hey, it happens to us all! Here is one of my favorite hangover cures that'll help settle your tum tum, and it's super delicious even when you're not hungover! :D

1 banana
1 pear (green or red is fine!)
2/3 c almond milk
2-4 pieces of sliced ginger
2 Tbsp honey
¼ tsp ground cinnamon
1 ½ c chopped kale
1 c ice

You don't have to peel the pear, but I would def recommend peeling the banana. Chop up the fruit into chunks and add everything into a blender. Blend for three minutes or until it's all sexy smooth and delicious. You can add more or less ginger, depending on your tasty buds. Ditto with the cinnamon. You can also add a few drops of vanilla extract!

If you know you're gonna be hungover in advance, I would prep this stuff the night before. Nothing sucks more than measuring out ingredients with a big ol' headache. :D :D :D

Recipes

PANDORA'S BLUEBERRY PIE

(coz Sloane says his mom is likely still pissed in the beyond about him using store-bought as an offering to the gods that Dhankes he first met Loch)

× Pie dough for top and bottom, chilled, about 9-inches nice! :)
× 3/4 cup granulated sugar
× 1/4 cup cornstarch
× 2 teaspoons freshly grated lemon zest
× 1/8 teaspoon ground allspice
× 1/8 teaspoon ground cinnamon
× 1/8 teaspoon salt
× 2 pounds fresh blueberries (about 6 cups)
× 1 tablespoon butter, cut into small squares
× 1 egg
× 1 tablespoon heavy cream
× 1 tablespoon coarse sugar (demerara works great!)

could make the pie dough from scratch too, but store bought is just as good and comes in a two-pack.

Sloane's mom wouldn't be too mad, would she?

Yes.

PREPARE BOTTOM: never skip this step :D

Press one part of pie crest into bottom of pan before adding filling, and save other for top, which you can rip into pieces for a lattice look, or leave flat—but if you leave it, make sure to cut slits throughout for it to 'breathe'.

P.S. Loch says not doing it the lattice way is sacrilege

FILLING:

Stir sugar, cornstarch, lemon peel, allspice, cinnamon, and salt in a large bowl. Add blueberries and gently toss to combine. Transfer blueberry filling to prepared crust.

TO FINISH: coz who doesn't want that!

Heat oven to 400 degrees F. Finish top crust while it heats. Dot melted butter over the open areas of the lattice, and then whisk egg and cream together to brush over the dough, finally sprinkling coarse sugar over the entire top. Then bake 20 minutes. Reduce heat to 350 and continue to bake 35 to 45 minutes, or until crust is golden and juices in filling are bubbling.

Cool 2 to 3 hours before serving.

Loch says best served cold next day with ice cream, yum!

Loch is an idiot.

Neun Monde Cake

CAKE:

- × 4 large eggs
- × 1/2 teaspoon salt
- × 1 cup granulated sugar
- × 1 cup sour cream
- × 14 oz dulce de leche, 1 can
- × 1 teaspoon baking soda
- × 2 cups flour
- × 2 teaspoons baking powder

You do NOT need a baby to enjoy this cake. Just in case that's not clear. No baby required. That would be super weird if it was.

SYRUP:

- × 8 teaspoons of tears from an Asra fermented for 8 weeks minimum*
- × 14 oz dulce de leche, 1 can

CREAM:

- × 8 oz butter, unsalted, room temperature
- × 8 oz cream cheese, room temperature
- × 14 oz dulce de leche, 1 can
- × 16 oz whipped topping or heavy whipping cream

*yikes! I guess evaporated milk is a suitable replacement – also, I was warned to not make other comments on this one or risk heavenly wrath, so...

Preheat oven to 350 degrees F with baking rack in middle. Line 2 large baking sheet pans with parchment or silicone mats & set aside. You can also butter and flour the sheet pans instead.

Whip together 4 eggs, 1 cup sugar, and 1/2 teaspoon salt for about 10 minutes. When eggs are almost done, in a separate medium bowl whisk together 1 cup sour cream, 1 can dulce de leche and 1 teaspoon of baking soda until no lumps of dulce de leche are seen. Fold the two mixtures together, being careful not to overmix and deflate the batter.

Sift in 2 cups of flour and 2 teaspoons of baking powder, then fold batter until fully incorporated. Do not overmix or cake will be tough. Divide batter between the 2 prepared baking sheets into an even layer. Bake for 9 minutes, or until the top is lightly golden and springs back when touched, or when toothpick comes out clean.

While cake cools, make syrup by combining evaporated milk and dulce de leche until smooth. Then, for cream, if using heavy whipping cream instead of whipped topping, whip cream with a mixer until medium peaks form and refrigerate.

Next, whip 8 oz of cubed room temperature butter and 8 oz cubed cream cheese for 4-5 minutes or until mixture is fluffy. Add final dulce de leche, and then fold in whipped cream/whipped topping.

Cut cakes in half to have 4 equal layers. Reserve about 2 cups of cream and set aside. Layer the cake by soaking each layer in the syrup, then spreading some cream. Repeat with other layers, then use reserved cream to cover top and sides of cake. Refrigerate for 2-3 hours before serving.

OLLIE'S FLUFFY SCRAMBLED EGGS

(hey, that's me!)

- × 4 large eggs
- × 1 tablespoon milk
- × Shredded cheese
- × Salt and pepper
- × Sriracha

ideal for two hungry people; add same amount for more hungry people or double that for hungry gods – oh and sharp cheddar is like the best ever. And Sriracha is optional but nom.

Whisk eggs in a bowl with milk, salt and pepper. Lightly grease medium-hot skillet, with oil or butter (or a combination of oil and butter). Pour eggs into skillet.

Mix eggs as they begin to cook. When about halfway done, add cheese. Turn off heat when eggs are 90% done to prevent overcooking and add Sriracha for added spice and flavor. Serve immediately.

Use pepper jack cheese.

No, cheddar is better

Pepper jack.

CHEDDAR.

Pepper jack.

CHEDDAR

PEPPER JACK! LOOK SEE I CAN WRITE IN ALL CAPITALS TOO

You have really pretty handwriting <333

Ugh. Just make mine with pepper jack, please.

ASRAN SOUS VIDE STEAK

× 1 sirloin steak (1 pound, about 1 inch thick)*
× 1/2 teaspoon coarse salt
× 1/2 teaspoon black pepper
× 1 tablespoon olive oil, divided
× 2 cloves garlic, minced
× fresh rosemary

*as big as your head if you can find it, but like, seriously, size doesn't ALWAYS matter

Preheat sous vide water bath: Add water to sous vide container or a large pot, set sous vide precision cooker to 135 degrees F for medium-rare doneness. Rub steak with 1/2 tablespoon oil on all sides. Season both sides with salt, pepper, garlic, and rosemary.

Add seasoned sirloin to zip-lock bag. Seal all but one corner of bag, and slowly place in water bath. Make sure everything below the zip-line is covered by water, then seal the rest of the bag. Use a kitchen tong to help push down bag if water is too hot.

Cook for 1 hour for a 1-inch sirloin steak. (1.5 hours for 1.5 inches, 2 hours for 2 inches, and so on) When timer goes off, remove steak from bag and wipe off moisture with paper towels. Season with more salt and pepper if necessary.

Heat cast-iron skillet on medium-high. Add remaining oil. Once hot, add steak and sear about 1 minute per side.

Almost as good as if prepared by an immortal king of cats :D

STEAMY ROAST

Perfect for a growing godly fetus :D :D :D

- × 3-5 pound well-marbled chuck roast
- × Salt and pepper
- × 2 tablespoons oil
- × 1 large onion
- × 1 cup red wine
- × 2 cups beef broth
- × 1 tablespoon Worcestershire sauce*
- × 4 garlic cloves, smashed or minced
- × 3 sprigs fresh rosemary
- × 3 sprigs fresh thyme
- × 6 medium carrots, peeled and chopped
- × 2 pounds potatoes, peeled
- × 2 pounds mushrooms

*or Sriracha if you don't enjoy Worcestershire

Preheat oven to 275 degrees F. Generously season chuck roast with salt and pepper. Heat oil in cast iron over medium-high. Sear meat on all sides, until browned all over. Set aside.

With burner still on medium-high, add onions and cook 1-2 minutes. Add wine and scrape bottom to deglaze. Add roast back in, beef broth, and Worcestershire. (or Sriracha.)

Place garlic and fresh herbs on top of roast. Cover and place in oven. While roast begins to cook, peel carrots and potatoes, and wash mushrooms. Once vegetables are fully prepped, remove pot from oven and place vegetables on top of beef. Cover and return to oven.

Cook until roast is fall-apart tender, usually 3-4 hours, depending on the size of your meat. (hehehe meeeeat)

THE FIRST DHANKES CAKE

CAKE INGREDIENTS:

- × 1 2/3 cup all-purpose flour
- × 1 cup granulated sugar
- × 1 tsp baking powder
- × 1/4 tsp baking soda
- × 1 cup whole milk (or your favorite milk)
- × 2 tablespoons black vanilla tea
- × 1/2 tsp culinary lavender
- × 3/4 cup unsalted butter, almost melted
- × 1/2 cup sour cream
- × 3 tsp vanilla extract
- × 3 egg whites large

LAVENDER MILK:

- × 2 1/2 cups unsweetened vanilla almond milk (or your favorite milk)
- × 1 tablespoon honey
- × 1/2 a whole vanilla bean
- × 1 tablespoon culinary lavender, wrapped in cheesecloth

Preheat oven to 350 degrees F. Grease 9x13 pan.

Sift dry ingredients (including sugar). In a small saucepan over medium heat, combine milk, culinary lavender, and black tea. Let simmer for about 10 minutes, then cool.

In medium bowl, combine wet ingredients, including butter and 1/2 cup of infused milk. Combine wet and dry mixtures. Pour into pan and bake for 30-35 minutes or until center is set and springy to the touch.

FOR LAVENDER MILK BATH:

Place milk, honey, and vanilla bean in a small saucepan over medium heat. Add lavender sachet to milk and bring to heavy simmer. Turn off heat and let cool slightly. Pour over warm cake for desired moistness.

Heheheee. Moist.

Also. This step can totally be skipped if you just want to enjoy yummy cake and don't have the culinary perfection of a goddess.

GODLY (AND DETECTIVE-Y?) SPAGHETTI

- × 1 pound spicy Italian sausage
- × 1 pound lean ground beef
- × 1 large onion, diced
- × 5 cloves garlic, minced
- × 2 tablespoons granulated sugar
- × 2 teaspoons dried Italian seasoning
- × 1 teaspoon salt
- × 1/2 teaspoon pepper
- × 1/3 cup fresh chopped parsley
- × 12 ounces tomato paste
- × 15 ounce can diced fire-roasted tomatoes
- × 28 ounce can crushed tomatoes
- × 1/2 cup chicken broth

In large pot or pan, cook sausage and beef over medium-high heat. Add in onion and garlic, stirring constantly, until meat is browned. Drain off fat.

Reduce heat to medium; add in sugar, Italian seasoning, salt, pepper, and parsley. Add in tomato paste and stir to combine. Pour in diced tomatoes, crushed tomatoes, and chicken broth.

Stir well until combined; bring to a simmer, then reduce heat to low and simmer for at least 1 hour. (or as long as hungry gods, detectives, and translators are willing to wait)

Serve over spaghetti noodles or other noodles of your choice. Don't forget the frozen breadsticks!

GODDESS APPROVED CHICKEN SOUP

(for Starkiller morning sickness)

- × 1 roasted chicken 3-5 lbs
- × 1 1/2 cups dried seaweed
- × 1 tsbp olive oil
- × 1/2 yellow onion, chopped
- × 4 stalks celery, chopped
- × 1 cup carrots, sliced into coins
- × 1 inch grated ginger
- × 1/2 large fennel bulb, sliced into small chunks, fronds discarded
- × 3 pints chicken bone broth
- × 2 cups water
- × 1 1/2 teaspoon white pepper
- × 3 tablespoons sweet white miso

Place seaweed in medium pot, cover with water and simmer for 10 minutes. Strain and set aside.

In a large pot over med-high heat, sauté onions, celery, and carrots in olive oil for 5-7 minutes. Add ginger and fennel, stir and sauté another 2 minutes. Add chicken bone broth and water. Bring to boil, then lower and simmer, covered.

Remove roasted chicken meat from bone and chop into small pieces. Add chicken and seaweed to pot. Sprinkle in white pepper. Remove from heat and stir in miso. Taste for seasoning and enjoy.

UNFAILABLE CHEESE SOUFFLE

(well... I guess Loch's still working on this one!)

- × 1/4 cup plus 2 tablespoons freshly grated Parmigiano-Reggiano cheese
- × 3 tablespoons unsalted butter
- × 3 tablespoons all-purpose flour
- × 1 1/4 cups heavy cream
- × 4 large eggs, separated, plus 3 large egg whites
- × 3 tablespoons dry sherry
- × 6 ounces shredded Gruyère cheese
- × 2 tablespoons sour cream
- × 1 1/4 teaspoons salt
- × 1 teaspoon Dijon mustard
- × 1/2 teaspoon dry mustard
- × 1/4 teaspoon cayenne pepper
- × 1/4 teaspoon cream of tartar

Preheat oven to 375 degrees F. Butter a 1 1/2-quart soufflé dish and coat with 2 tablespoons of Parmigiano. In medium saucepan, melt butter. Stir in flour to make a paste. Gradually whisk in cream and bring to a boil over moderate heat.

Reduce heat to low and cook, whisking, until very thick, about 3 minutes. Transfer base to a large bowl; let cool. Stir in egg yolks, sherry, Gruyère, sour cream, salt, Dijon mustard, dry mustard, cayenne and remaining 1/4 cup Parmigiano.

Put 7 egg whites in large stainless steel bowl. Add cream of tartar. Using electric mixer, beat whites until firm peaks form. Fold one-third of whites into soufflé base to lighten it, then fold in remaining whites until no streaks remain.

Scrape mixture into prepared dish. Run your thumb around inside rim of dish to wipe away any crumbs. Bake about 35 minutes, until soufflé is golden brown and puffed.

Serve right away.

If it fails, roast it with godly dragon fire!

BETTER LOCH NEXT TIME COOKIES

× 3/4 cup (3/4 stick) Butter Flavor Crisco Shortening**

**NOT butter or other Crisco or it's just wrong

× 1 1/4 cups firmly packed light brown sugar
× 2 tablespoons milk
× 1 tablespoon vanilla
× 1 egg
× 1 3/4 cups all-purpose flour
× 1 teaspoon salt
× 3/4 teaspoon baking soda
× 1 cup chocolate chips

semi-sweet, milk, or dark, as preferred, but semi-sweet is totally the best—trust in the gods (or at least trust Loch) XD XD

Preheat oven to 375 degrees F. Combine Crisco, brown sugar, milk, and vanilla in large bowl. Beat at medium speed until well blended. Beat egg into creamed mixture. Combine flour, salt, and baking soda. Mix into creamed mixture until blended. Stir in chocolate chips.

Drop rounded spoonfuls of dough onto ungreased baking sheet. Bake one sheet at a time for 8-10 minutes.

Best if made with fire extinguisher nearby just to be safe.

Makes about 3 dozen cookies.
(assuming you don't burn them like Loch does)

K.L. "KAT" HIERS is an embalmer, restorative artist, and queer writer. Licensed in both funeral directing and funeral service, they worked in the death industry for nearly a decade. Their first love was always telling stories, and they have been writing for over twenty years, penning their very first book at just eight years old. Publishers generally do not accept manuscripts in Hello Kitty notebooks, however, but they never gave up.

Following the success of their first novel, Cold Hard Cash, they now enjoy writing professionally, focusing on spinning tales of sultry passion, exotic worlds, and emotional journeys. They love attending horror movie conventions and indulging in cosplay of their favorite characters. They live in Zebulon, NC, with their family, including their children, some of whom have paws and a few that only pretend to because they think it's cute.

Website: http://www.klhiers.com

Follow me on BookBub

JOHN T. FULLER hails from the north of England, where he lives with his partner. He works with computers by day, writes by night, and enjoys real ale, classic rock, and doing the odd bit of illustration. You can pick up a copy of his novella *When the Music Stops* or his short story collection *The Trojan Project* (jointly authored with Richard Rider) online. He's currently working on a historical romance set during the English Civil War. He hangs out at https://www.goodreads.com/john_t_fuller and cannot promise not to put sausages on all of his book covers.

By K.L. Hiers

SUCKER FOR LOVE MYSTERIES
Acsquidentally In Love
Kraken My Heart
Head Over Tentacles
Nautilus Than Perfect
Just Calamarried
Our Shellfish Desires
Insquidious Devotion
Ollie's Octrageously Official Omnibus

Published by Dreamspinner Press
www.dreamspinnerpress.com

A SUCKER FOR LOVE MYSTERY

ACSQUIDENTALLY
IN LOVE

K.L. HIERS

A Sucker For Love Mystery

Nothing brings two men—or one man and an ancient god—together like revenge.

Private investigator Sloane sacrificed his career in law enforcement in pursuit of his parents' murderer. Like them, he is a follower of long-forgotten gods, practicing their magic and offering them his prayers… not that he's ever gotten a response.

Until now.

Azaethoth the Lesser might be the patron of thieves and tricksters, but he takes care of his followers. He's come to earth to avenge the killing of one of his favorites, and maybe charm the pants off the cute detective Fate has placed in his path. If he has his way, they'll do much more than bring a killer to justice. In fact, he's sure he's found the man he'll spend his immortal life with.

Sloane's resolve is crumbling under Azaethoth's surprising sweetness, and the tentacles he sometimes glimpses escaping the god's mortal form set his imagination alight. But their investigation gets stranger and deadlier with every turn. To survive, they'll need a little faith… and a lot of mystical firepower.

www.dreamspinnerpress.com

A SUCKER FOR LOVE MYSTERY

KRAKEN MY
HEART

K.L. HIERS

"A breezy and sensual LGBTQ paranormal romance."
—Library Journal, "Acsquidentally in Love"

A Sucker For Love Mystery

It's just Ted's luck that he meets the love of his life while covered in the blood of a murder victim.

Funeral worker Ted Sturm has a foul mouth, a big heart, and a knack for communicating with the dead. Unfortunately the dead don't make very good friends, and Ted's only living pal, his roommate, just rescued a strange cat who's determined to make his life even more miserable. This cat is more than he seems, and soon Ted finds himself in an alternate dimension… and on top of a dead body.

When Ted is accused of murder, his only ally in a strange world full of powerful magical beings calling for his head is King Grell, a sarcastic, randy, catlike immortal with impressive abilities… and anatomy. The two soon find themselves at the center of a cosmic conspiracy and surrounded by dangerous enemies. But with Ted's special skills and Grell's magic, they have a chance to get to the bottom of the mystery and save Ted. There's just one problem: Ted's got to resist Grell's aggressive advances… and he isn't sure he wants to.

www.dreamspinnerpress.com

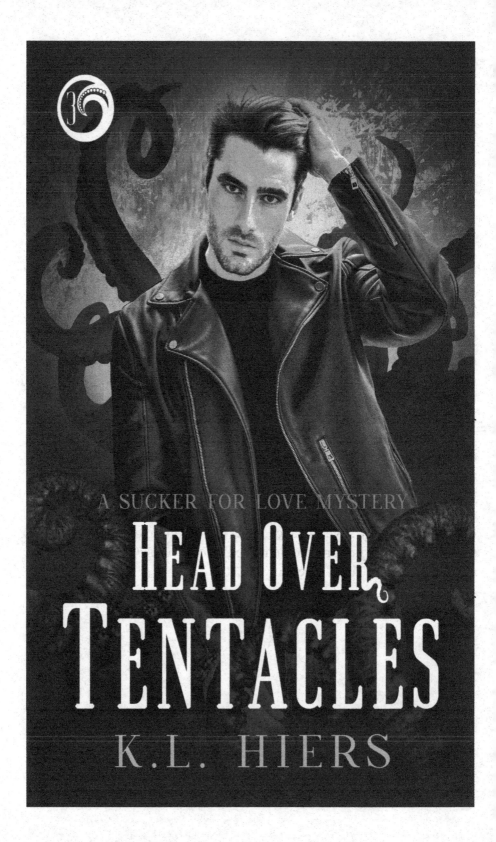

A SUCKER FOR LOVE MYSTERY

Head Over
Tentacles

K.L. HIERS

A Sucker For Love Mystery

Private investigator Sloane Beaumont should be enjoying his recent engagement to eldritch god Azaethoth the Lesser, AKA Loch. Unfortunately, he doesn't have time for a pre-honeymoon period.

The trouble starts with a deceptively simple missing persons case. That leads to the discovery of mass kidnappings, nefarious secret experiments, and the revelation that another ancient god is trying to bring about the end of the world by twisting humans into an evil army.

Just another day at the office.

Sloane does his best to juggle wedding planning, stopping his fiancé from turning the mailman inside out, and meeting his future godly in-laws while working the case, but they're also being hunted by a strange young man with incredible abilities. With the wedding date looming closer, Sloane and Loch must combine their powers to discover the truth—because it's not just their own happy-ever-after at stake, but the fate of the world....

www.dreamspinnerpress.com

A SUCKER FOR LOVE MYSTERY

NAUTILUS THAN PERFECT

K.L. HIERS

A Sucker For Love Mystery

Detective Elwood Q. Chase has ninety-nine problems, and the unexpected revelation that his partner is a god is only one of them.

Chase has been in love with Benjamin Merrick for years and has resigned himself to a life of unrequited pining. But when they run afoul of a strange cult, Merrick's secret identity as Gordoth the Untouched slips out… and so do Chase's feelings. The timing can't be helped, but now Merrick thinks Chase only cares about him because he's a god.

Even more unfortunately, it turns out the cultists want to perform a ritual to end the world. Chase's mission to convince Merrick his feelings predate any divine revelations takes a back seat to a case tangled with murder and lies, but Chase doesn't give up. Once he finds out there's a chance Merrick feels the same way, he digs in his heels. Suddenly he's trying to court a god and save the world at the same time. What could possibly go wrong?

www.dreamspinnerpress.com

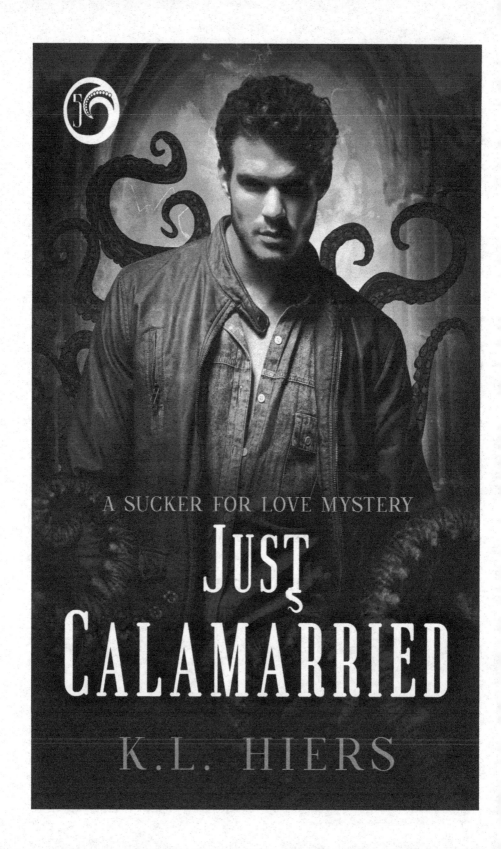

A SUCKER FOR LOVE MYSTERY

JUST
CALAMARRIED

K.L. HIERS

A Sucker For Love Mystery

Newlyweds Sloane and Loch are eagerly expecting their first child, though for Sloane that excitement is tempered by pregnancy side effects. Carrying a god's baby would be enough to deal with, especially with the whole accelerated gestation thing, but it's not like Sloane can take maternity leave. He works for himself as a private investigator. Which leads him to his next case.

At least this strange new mystery distracts him from the stress of constant puking.

When two priests are murdered within hours of each other, a woman named Daphne hires Sloane and Loch to track down the prime suspect— her brother—before the police do. Between untangling a conspiracy of lies and greed, going toe-to-toe with a gangster, and stealing a cat, they hardly have time to decorate a nursery....

www.dreamspinnerpress.com